# Frederick Douglass

*Illustrated by*
*Meryl Henderson*

# Frederick Douglass

## ABOLITIONIST HERO

*by George E. Stanley*

**ALADDIN PAPERBACKS**
New York   London   Toronto   Sydney

ALADDIN PAPERBACKS
An imprint of Simon & Schuster Children's Publishing Division
1230 Avenue of the Americas, New York, NY 10020
Text copyright © 2008 by George E. Stanley
Illustrations copyright © 2008 by Meryl Henderson
All rights reserved, including the right of reproduction
in whole or in part in any form.
ALADDIN PAPERBACKS, CHILDHOOD OF
FAMOUS AMERICANS and related logo are
registered trademarks of Simon & Schuster, Inc.
Designed by Lisa Vega
The text of this book was set in New Caledonia.
Manufactured in the United States of America
First Aladdin Paperbacks edition July 2008
4 6 8 10 9 7 5 3
Library of Congress Control Number 2007934395
ISBN-13: 978-1-4169-5547-4
ISBN-10: 1-4169-5547-X
0715 OFF

# Illustrations

# CONTENTS

# A Slave Child Is Born

One cold February morning in 1818, an old midwife delivered a baby and announced, "It's a boy, Miss Harriet!"

Harriet Bailey opened her eyes and looked up into the woman's winkled face. "Show him to me, please," she said.

Her mother stepped forward to see the baby. When the midwife held up the baby so Harriet could see him, she thought, *He does look like his father*. Harriet had overheard some of the other plantation slaves

talking about how they were sure the father was Captain Aaron Anthony, the white man who had been hired to manage Colonel Edward Lloyd's huge cotton plantation near Tuckahoe, Maryland, but Harriet had already decided that the secret would go with her to her grave.

Suddenly, Harriet shivered, and then her body began to shake uncontrollably, but she said, "I have to get up. I have to be in the fields before dawn. If I'm not, I'll be—"

"Hush, now, you'll be staying right where you are," the midwife said. "No one needs to know yet that the child has been born."

Harriet sank back into the thin blanket. She closed her eyes and tried to relax for a minute, but all she could think about was how she wouldn't be able to hold the baby for very long or nurse him after today. If she wanted to see him at all, she would have to walk several miles from the plantation where she worked to the little shack where her parents, Betsey and Isaac Bailey, lived. Because they were old and couldn't work in the fields, they took care of some of the children of the other slaves.

"Harriet?" her mother said.

Harriet opened her eyes again. "Yes, Mama?"

"Your boy needs to nurse, sweetheart," Mrs. Bailey said. She handed the baby to Harriet. "What are you going to name him?" she asked.

Without any hesitation, Harriet said, "Frederick Augustus Washington Bailey."

"That's a fine, sturdy name," Mrs. Bailey said, "but then he's a fine, sturdy boy."

"Mama, I know your friend Lizzy can read and write a little, so I want you to ask her to write down that Frederick was born in the year 1818, in Talbot County, Maryland, and then I want . . ."

But Harriet didn't finish her sentence. She drifted off to sleep, as Frederick continued to nurse.

● ● ●

Two days later, Mrs. Bailey had just helped Harriet stand up, when the overseer appeared at the door and said, "If you're not back in the fields by noon, woman, I'll whip you!"

"She'll be there, master," Mrs. Bailey said hurriedly. "She's just delivered, so she's still weak, but we'll make sure she's in the fields. It won't help if you beat her, because then she won't be able to work."

The overseer walked over to Mrs. Bailey and struck her. "Don't you ever sass me again, old woman!"

"Yes, sir," Mrs. Bailey said. "I didn't mean it, sir."

The overseer turned and left the shack. Harriet leaned on her mother's shoulder. "I'm sorry, Mama," she sobbed. "I should have left before. He had no right to do that to you."

"Yes, he did, Harriet," Mrs. Bailey said. "Mr. Lloyd owns us, and his overseer can do whatever he wants to."

•   •   •

Within the hour, Harriet left the shack. With a tearful good-bye, she let her mother take Frederick out of her arms. Just once, Harriet looked back and saw her mother standing in the doorway of the shack, holding Frederick. She whispered a silent prayer of thanks that she had her parents nearby, for she was one of the fortunate slaves. Most of the time, families were separated at slave auctions, with everyone going to different owners, scattered over the countryside.

The sky in the east had begun to lighten, forcing Harriet to quicken her step so she would be sure to be in the field by sunrise. She knew the overseer had not been making idle threats about whipping her if she didn't appear.

Over the next few months, when she could, Harriet would slip away from the slave quarters where she lived, ten miles away, and hurry along the dark paths that led to her parents' shack so she could be with her son.

"Oh my, how he's grown," Harriet would say in a hushed voice, trying not to wake Frederick, but he seemed to sense that his mother was there. He almost always opened his eyes and Harriet would see him smile at her. "My precious, precious boy," she would whisper to him. Then she would lie curled up on a blanket on the floor with Frederick until he fell asleep again, as she hummed a song. But Harriet would always have to leave to be in the fields by sunrise.

As the years passed, Frederick's grandparents were always around to love and take care of him. His mother still came at night, but she didn't come as often, and when she did come, she coughed a lot, and Frederick would often see a look of sadness in his grandmother's eyes.

"What's wrong with Mama?" Frederick would ask his grandmother, after his mother had left. His grandmother would always say, "Oh, she just misses you, that's all."

Frederick loved to play outside on hot summer days with the other children his age. They would chase one another into the woods, squealing at the top of their lungs, and then, after they were tired and sweaty, they would wade in the small creek that flowed nearby.

Frederick often overheard some of the older people talking about not having enough to eat, but this was something he didn't really understand. In the summers, Frederick searched for all the different kinds of berries his grandmother had told him about. When he found them, he would eat his fill, then he would take the cloth that his grandmother had tied around his waist and he'd gather as many of the remaining berries that he could carry to take home. In the autumn, Frederick would look for nuts on the ground.

It was in the winter, when it snowed or when the wind cut through his tattered, worn clothing, that life became more difficult. Sometimes, when it was really cold, Frederick even crawled into the corner of the fireplace and stuck his feet in the ashes. If he closed his eyes, he could believe that it was summer again, and that he was sitting on the bank of the creek, dangling his feet in the sun-warmed water.

Frederick seldom saw his mother now, because he had two more sisters, Kitty and Arianna, but his grandmother told him they were living closer to his mother.

Frederick's daily life continued in much the same way until one morning, in 1824, when he was almost six, when his grandmother awakened him and said, "Hurry up and get dressed. Today, I'm taking you to the Great House."

# The Great House

As they started down the dusty road toward the Great House, Frederick said, "How far is it, Grandma?"

"About twelve miles, more or less," his grandmother replied, "but I packed some food in case you get hungry."

Frederick decided he was hungry right then, so his grandmother gave him a corncake.

All the way there, Frederick tried to conjure up in his mind what the Great House would look like, but nothing he thought of prepared him for his first glimpse of the magnificent structure.

"It's beautiful," Frederick whispered, more to himself than to anyone else.

"Yes, it is, Frederick, my child," his grandmother said. "Yes, it is."

"Will I really be living there?" Frederick asked.

His grandmother nodded. "You're a fortunate young man, Frederick, and I don't want you ever to forget that either," she said. "You've been picked, son, and being picked means you'll be called a *servant* instead of a *slave*. If you do a good job for the master, you might stay in the Great House for the rest of your life." His grandmother stopped and sighed. "That's what you want, Frederick. That's what you want."

Once again, they walked. They were getting closer and closer to the Great House. All of a sudden Frederick began to feel uneasy about what his grandmother had just said to him. Until this very moment, being a slave owned by a white master—and all the terrible things that could happen to him—had just been part of a story he had heard from the other children he played with or from the adults who talked in whispers to his grandparents. Now, it was suddenly very real, and Frederick wasn't at all sure that he wanted to stay at the Great House for the rest of his life.

But he said, "Yes, Grandmother. I promise I'll be good and do what the master tells me to, and I won't give him any trouble."

Now, they were passing by the dairy, the greenhouses, the washhouses, and the kitchens. Frederick had never seen so many people.

"This is the greatest plantation in Maryland, son," his grandmother said. "There are thousands of folks who live and work here."

Up ahead, Frederick saw several wire pens with turkeys, pigeons, and chickens. He ran to them. "Look, Grandma!" he said. "Will I get to eat these when I live in the Great House?"

His grandmother shook her head. "Now, son, don't get it in your head that a lot is going to change all at once," she said. "You're still a slave, and you'll still be eating your corn mush and leftover scraps and liking it. If the master takes to you, then I hear tell that things will get better."

Frederick's mouth began to water. Often, when he had been running around the woods, near his grandparents' shack, he would sneak up close to some of the kitchens and smell the food cooking. Once, he had even asked one of the old cooks what that good smell was, and she had told him it was fried chicken. Frederick had never forgotten it. Right then, he vowed that he would be so good at whatever the master at the Great House asked him to do that the cook would certainly give him meat to eat.

"We have to hurry, Frederick," his grandmother said.

"Yes, ma'am," Frederick said. He took his

grandmother's hand, and they started down the road again. "But one of these days, I promise you," Frederick said, "I'm going to eat anything I want to eat, and I'm going to make sure you and Grandpa do too."

Suddenly, Frederick stopped. Up ahead, he saw several houses just like the one he had left. "I thought everything would be nicer at the Great House."

"Oh, it is, Frederick, it is, at the *Great House*, son," his grandmother replied, squeezing his hand, "but a slave's house is a slave's house, no matter what plantation it's on, if those slaves work in the fields."

Two girls and a boy started running toward them, shouting their names.

"How do they know who we are, Grandma?" Frederick asked.

"Because the two girls are your sisters, Sarah and Eliza, and the boy is your brother, Perry," his grandmother said. "They must have heard we were coming."

14

Frederick squeezed his grandmother's hand harder and grabbed her dress with the other hand.

"Now, Frederick, sweetheart, there's no need to be afraid," his grandmother said. "They're your own flesh and blood, and that's mighty unheard of for most slaves to be with family. I want you to be happy."

"All right," Frederick said. Inside, though, he wasn't at all sure that he was going to be happy.

When Perry, Sarah, and Eliza reached them, they linked arms and circled Frederick and Grandmother Bailey, singing, "We saw you coming! We saw you coming!"

"Well, how did you know to look for us?" Grandmother Bailey asked.

"Old Peter told us," Sarah said. "He's too old to work in the fields anymore, but he still knows everything that happens around here."

"Well, I have to talk to some people at the Great House," Grandmother Bailey said.

"Perry, why don't you show your brother around so he'll know something about his new home. You two girls can come with me."

Perry took Frederick's hand and started to pull him back down the road, but Frederick stood his ground.

"I don't want to go, Grandma," Frederick cried. "I want to stay with you."

His grandmother wrapped her arms around him and held him close. Frederick could hear the beat of her heart. She bent down close to his ear and whispered, "I love you with all my heart, son, and I always will. Now, you've been given a chance to live in the Great House. I want you to look forward to that, not backward, to your old grandma and grandpa. You're going to go with your brother, Perry, here, so you'll know how to start your new life. You're something special. Your grandmother will always be here for you, Frederick, always, so you never forget that."

Frederick swallowed hard. No one had

ever talked to him like that before, but there was something in his grandmother's voice that had calmed him. He hugged her tight, kissed her wrinkled cheek, and then said, "All right, Grandma. I love you."

"I love you, too, son," his grandmother said. "Always and forever."

Frederick let Perry take his hand and pull him down the road, but once, when he looked back, Frederick saw his two sisters jumping up and down, stirring up the dust, tugging at his grandmother's dress, but his grandmother wasn't really paying attention to what they were doing. She was looking at Frederick. She nodded her head ever so slightly, and Frederick turned around to listen to what Perry was telling him.

"See that red house over there?" Perry said.

Frederick nodded.

"Well, you want to steer clear of it always," Perry said, "because that's where Mr. Severe lives, and you don't ever want to make Mr. Severe angry."

"Why not?" Frederick asked.

"Are you crazy, boy?" Perry said. He had stopped and put his hands on his hips. "He's an overseer, but he's the one who always carries a large hickory stick, and he'll whip you if you just look at him wrong."

Frederick shuddered.

"I won't look at him, ever," Frederick promised.

"Well, you'll be living in the Great House, anyway, so he probably won't bother you," Perry said. "He's worse after he's been drinking, so just try to stay away."

Just then Sarah and Eliza ran up to them. "Grandma Bailey's gone, Frederick. She's gone. After you left, she just stood there crying. She told us to make sure that you don't try to follow her."

All at once, Frederick was overwhelmed by what was happening. Even though his grandmother had prepared him for this moment, he suddenly couldn't imagine life without her. He fell to the ground and started sobbing.

Perry nudged him with his foot. "You'd better get up, boy, because if Mr. Severe sees you, he'll whip you before you can tell him you're not a fieldhand."

"Leave me alone," Frederick said.

"It's true, Frederick," Sarah said. "He'll do it."

Frederick pushed himself up slowly. "He'd better not touch me," he said. "He'd better never lay a hand on me!"

"You'd better stop talking like that," Eliza said. "He'll do it for sure now."

Frederick stood up all the way and dusted himself off. "I'm going back," he said. "I don't want to live at the Great House."

"Don't you know anything?" Perry shouted. "You're a slave, and you can't decide what you're going to do and what you're not going to do."

20

"If you go back, they'll whip Grandmother, too," Sarah said. "She was told to bring you to the Great House, and that's what she did, so you'd better stop crying, so we can present you to the master."

Frederick took one more look down the road where he had last seen his grandmother. "All right," he said. "I'm ready. Take me to the Great House."

# Why Are People So Mean to Each Other?

Frederick soon discovered that his brother knew almost everything that went on at the plantation.

"Remember this, Frederick. You have two masters," Perry told him. "Captain Anthony and his overseer, Mr. Plummer. Captain Anthony is Colonel Lloyd's clerk and superintendent. He oversees the overseers."

Frederick wanted to tell Perry to slow down, that he couldn't keep up with everything he was saying, but he knew it was important to find out all he could before Perry left him. He had no idea how long it would be before he saw his brother again.

"Since you'll be working in the Great House, you probably won't have to worry about Mr. Plummer," Perry continued, "but he goes there from time to time. If he does, make sure you're nowhere around."

"Why?" Frederick asked.

"Why? Well, I'm going to tell you why, brother," Perry said. "If you anger him, he'll never forget it, and he'll try to figure out some way for you to anger Captain Anthony so you'll have to go to the fields. That's when he'll take the whip to you."

Frederick shuddered. "I'll try to make sure that never happens," he said.

At first, all Frederick thought about was finding a way to return to his grandmother. But soon, he was so busy with his chores that his other life became only a distant memory. At night, he would cry himself to sleep. But one night, after Frederick had watched from the windows of the Great House as the other slaves went to the fields at dawn and came back at dusk, Frederick stopped crying. They always looked tired, as though they could hardly put one foot in front of the other. He knew they had had very little to eat, just small pieces of meat or fish, along with the horrid ash cakes, bread covered with ashes from being cooked in the embers of the fireplace.

*There's a reason my life is better than some of the other slaves'*, Frederick told himself. *I'll work hard and try to discover what it is.*

"Frederick?"

Frederick turned around. Captain Anthony's daughter, Lucretia, had come into the room. "Yes, ma'am?" he said.

"I've been looking all over for you," Lucretia said. "I need you to take some molasses to Mrs. Plummer."

Frederick could feel the blood draining

from his face. He started to shake. "When did you want me to go, Mrs. Lucretia?" he finally managed to ask.

"Now, Frederick," Lucretia replied. "She's mixing up some sulfur and molasses for one of her houseboys. It seems he has worms really bad."

"Yes, ma'am," Frederick said.

"Oh, yes, and here's a jar of salve, too," Lucretia added with a sigh. "Mr. Plummer whipped one of the fieldhands too hard, and his lashes have gotten infected."

"What did he do?" Frederick asked.

Lucretia blinked. "What?"

"What did the fieldhand do so that Mr. Plummer whipped him?" Frederick said.

"Well, Frederick, I'm surprised at you. I'm not used to being questioned like this," Lucretia said. She took a deep breath, and Frederick waited for her to lash out at him, but she only let out another sigh and said, "He was probably late coming to the field.

That's why they're usually punished, but it's none of your concern. Take these things to Mrs. Plummer and hurry back, because you have your other chores to do."

"Yes, ma'am, Mrs. Lucretia," Frederick said.

Lucretia had put both the salve and the molasses-and-sulfur mixture inside a cloth bag, which she handed to Frederick. Just as Frederick started to leave the room, Lucretia said, "Thank you!"

"You're welcome, ma'am," Frederick said. "I'll hurry back so I can do all my chores."

"All right," Lucretia said.

Frederick hurried to the backstairs and took them two at a time. Once outside, he started down a pathway he knew would lead to the Plummers' house. Frederick hoped there would be no chance of his encountering Mr. Plummer and his whip.

"Frederick!"

Frederick stopped and whirled around.

Isaac, one of Captain Anthony's prized servants, was standing at the entrance to the plantation's orchard. His hands were on his hips.

"Come here, Frederick," Isaac said.

Frederick ran up to him.

"Where are you going?" Isaac demanded.

"On an errand for Mrs. Lucretia," Frederick told him.

"You need to be in here chasing these birds away," Isaac said. "I have more important things to do."

"I'll be right back," Frederick said. "I don't want to stay long at the Plummers'."

"Lordy, boy, that's the truth," Isaac said. "Well, you hurry on up now, and get back here."

When Frederick reached the Plummers' house, he sprinted onto the porch and knocked. Within a few minutes the door was opened by a huge black woman Frederick had never seen before, who said, "What do you mean coming to the front like this, boy? You go around to the back like you know you should!" With that, she slammed the door in Frederick's face.

Frederick could feel the anger rising inside him. What difference did it make which door he went to? But he did what he was told.

When Frederick got to the back door, the big black woman was already there waiting for him.

"It's about time," she said. "I don't have all day."

"Mrs. Lucretia sent this—" Frederick started to say, but the woman interrupted him.

"I know what's in the bag, boy!" She grabbed it from him and once again slammed the door in his face.

Frederick took a deep breath and gritted his teeth. How could he control his anger, he wondered, when people he had never done anything bad to treated him this way?

When he got back to the orchard, Isaac said, "What took you so long?"

"I hurried as fast as I could," Frederick told him.

"Well, you know what you're supposed to do here, Frederick. Keep these awful birds from eating all of the fruits and vegetables," Isaac said.

"Isaac, why do people you've never done anything to treat you so unkindly?" Frederick interrupted.

"What are you talking about, boy?" Isaac asked.

"That woman who opened the door at the Plummers' house told me to go around back, before I had even said anything," Frederick explained. "And then when I did, she snatched the cloth bag with the molasses and salve from me and slammed the door in my face."

"Oh, that's just Old Bessie. She's not angry with you, son," Isaac said, "but she lives in that evil house, and when you're surrounded

by evil all the time, you're just out of sorts. Don't pay her no mind."

"Why can't people just be nice to other people?" Frederick said.

"Son, you're talking nonsense now, and Isaac here doesn't have any time for nonsense talk," Isaac said. Two crows landed in the asparagus, and he shooed them away. "Now, you listen to me, and you listen good. Just forget all of these ideas about people being nice to people, because you're a slave, and you'll always be a slave. What white folks tell you to do, you'd better do without even thinking about, let alone questioning. Right now, what you're supposed to be doing is scaring off these birds."

Frederick bowed his head, and Isaac put a hand on his shoulder. "Mrs. Lucretia didn't eat all of her bacon this morning, so I put it back for you, Frederick, and if you scare off all these birds, I'll give it to you."

"Thank you, Isaac," Frederick said.

"But I meant what I said," Isaac added, trying to sound stern. "If you don't do a good job, then I'll just have to eat it myself."

Frederick grinned. "Oh, don't worry, I'll make sure I'm the one who gets to eat the bacon."

Isaac laughed and headed back toward the Great House. Frederick watched him until a couple of crows decided to use the tall corn as perches, and then he ran toward them, shouting, "Shoo! Shoo! Shoo!"

Frederick was alone. One of the things he enjoyed about his job shooing birds out of the garden was that there was nobody to tell him what to do.

The apples hanging from the trees seemed to be begging someone to eat them. Just looking at their reddening skins made Frederick's mouth water, but one of the hard-and-fast rules of plantation life was that the food in the gardens was off-limits to slaves.

"They'll beat you within an inch of your life,

Frederick," Isaac had warned him, "if you so much as even touch one of those apples."

"How would they know?" Frederick asked.

"Oh, they'd know, and I'm not exactly sure how," Isaac replied, "but sometimes I think that Mr. Plummer comes out here late at night and counts the apples and counts the asparagus and counts the beans so that if he finds any missing, he'll have a reason to whip somebody."

Frederick wasn't sure if Isaac was serious about how anyone would know if he had eaten an apple, unless they found the core, and he'd be sure to hide it, but he'd heard how other slaves were caught. Mr. Lloyd put tar on the fences around the gardens so he would know that any slave with tar his clothes had climbed over the fences to steal food.

Frederick knew that he'd never get tar on his clothes, because he was supposed to be in the garden. That was his job. Anyway, he had vowed never to steal any of the food. First of all, it was wrong, and second of all, it would just be another thing that might send him to the fields, where Mr. Plummer could whip him.

Over the next few months, Frederick settled into what was almost a comfortable routine, which made him feel guilty, especially when he saw how most of the other slaves were treated. Several times, on errands for Mrs. Lucretia, he'd pass by shacks where older slave women were taking care of the younger children. If it was feeding time, he'd see their food being dumped into troughs, similar to those used for animals, and would watch how the children got down on their knees and, with their heads in the trough, gobbled down the food as fast as they could.

Quite often, some of the younger children were pushed aside, much as Frederick had seen pigs push aside the runts. He knew that night they'd go to bed hungry, their empty stomachs growling. Frederick would clinch his fists in anger but continue on his errand, all the while trying to think of a way he could stop all of this.

One fall day, when Frederick was in the garden, chasing crows away from the pumpkins, he heard footsteps behind him. He whirled around to see a white man looking at him.

"I wasn't doing anything wrong, sir," Frederick said.

"I never said you were," the man said. "Do you know who I am?"

"No, sir," Frederick said.

"I'm Daniel Lloyd," the man said. He waved his hand in a complete circle. "My father owns all of this, and that means he owns you, too."

"Yes, sir," Frederick said.

"Mrs. Lucretia said I could borrow you," Daniel said. "I want you to go hunting with me."

"I don't know how to hunt, sir," Frederick said.

"Of course, you don't," Daniel said. "You'll just be fetching the birds I shoot for me."

"Yes, sir," Frederick said.

Several times a week, for the next month, Frederick accompanied Daniel into the woods, and when Daniel shot a bird, usually a pheasant or duck, Frederick would retrieve it.

"You're better than any hound I've ever had," Daniel told him often.

"Thank you, sir," Frederick would say, but he wasn't sure being compared to a dog was anything he should be proud of. Still, he actually enjoyed being with Daniel. In the woods, away from the rest of the plantation, he was reminded of when he was still living with his grandmother and how he and his friends would chase one another through the trees.

In the evenings, after a hunt, Frederick would lie on his blanket, near the hearth in a backroom, and think about how it would be if he were no longer a slave. He liked the feeling he got, but he knew that he could never share it with anyone, including Isaac, so he kept it to himself. He knew that one of these days, though, he would go into the woods, maybe even when he was hunting with Daniel, and that he would never come back. In fact, he was sure of it.

"Frederick!"

Frederick opened his eyes. In the dimness of the room, he couldn't see anyone, but then, after a few minutes, a head peered around a corner. It was his brother, Perry.

"What are you doing here?" Frederick whispered. "You'll get whipped if they find you."

"I know, but I'm delivering a message from Grandmother," Perry said.

Frederick jumped up. "Is she here?" he asked.

Perry shook his head. "No," he said. "She sent it by Old Jimmy."

"What's the message?" Frederick asked.

"Our mother's sick," Perry said. "She's dying."

Frederick just looked at Perry, not knowing what he was supposed to say, but just as he opened his mouth, Perry disappeared, and when Frederick looked around the corner and through the door, Perry was gone.

Later that morning, Frederick told Lucretia that his mother was sick and that he thought he should go see her, but Lucretia told him that he couldn't do that because he was needed at the Great House.

A few months later, Perry appeared once again to tell Frederick that their mother had died.

"But I wanted to see her again, Perry," Frederick said. He fought to choke back the tears, but they came, anyway.

"Why?" Perry asked.

"I sort of remember her when I was little, and she came to Grandmother's house to be with me," Frederick told him.

"Well, she's dead now, boy, and that's all there is to it," Perry said. Without another word, he turned and left the room.

Frederick dried his eyes and went to look for Lucretia. She was in her sitting room.

"Ma'am," Frederick said, "my mother died, and I want to go see her buried."

Lucretia looked up slowly and said, "Frederick, don't you have chores to do?"

Frederick nodded. "Yes, ma'am," he said.

"Then why are you in here, bothering me with such nonsense? Can't you see that I'm busy with my embroidery?"

"Yes, ma'am," Frederick said, "but I just—"

Lucretia stopped him with a glare. "Don't you dare talk back to me! Now, you do what I told you to do!"

Frederick left the sitting room but stood outside for a few minutes, breathing deeply, trying to calm his anger. Frederick told himself that one day, he would escape from slavery.

# Stay Away from Austin Gore!

As best as Frederick could calculate, he was seven and a half years old today. Lucretia showed him a calendar on which the days and months of a year were written.

"There are sixty minutes in an hour, and there are twenty-four hours in a day, Frederick," she told him, "and there are thirty or thirty-one days in a month, except for February, which sometimes has twenty-eight or twenty-nine, and there are twelve months in a year, and then we start all over again."

"I want to be as smart as you are, Mrs. Lucretia," Frederick said, still marveling at how much she knew.

Lucretia laughed gently. "Well, Frederick, I'm not exactly sure how that will come to be," she said, "but you do seem to be more—intelligent than some of the other boys we've had in the house, so I'm sure you'll pick up little bits of information from time to time." She hesitated. "But . . . you'd do well to keep all of the information to yourself."

"Yes, ma'am," Frederick said.

A few weeks later, just as Frederick was waking up to the crowing of a nearby rooster, Isaac slipped into his room, his eyes wide with fear. Right away, Frederick was sure that he had done something wrong and that his life in the Great House was coming to an end.

"What's wrong?" Frederick asked.

Isaac said, "It's terrible, Frederick, it's

just terrible. Mr. Austin Gore is coming to the Great House as an overseer."

Frederick sat up, his heart pounding. "I've heard people talking awful about him before," he said. "Why is he coming to the Great House?"

"That's what we're all wondering," Isaac said. "Some of us think that Mr. Lloyd wants this overseer to be meaner."

"I didn't think anyone could be meaner than the other overseers," Frederick said. "They were evil men."

"Oh, if the truth be told, Frederick, they were just the devil's sons," Isaac said, "but Mr. Austin Gore is the devil himself, for sure."

Frederick shuddered.

"You'd better get up and get around, son," Isaac said. "I know it's earlier than usual, but it's best we're all working hard when Mr. Austin Gore comes by. If he sees one of us slacking off, he might tell Mr. Lloyd to take us out to the fields and whip us if we don't do what we're supposed to do."

With that, Frederick jumped up, dressed quickly, and washed his eyes in a cup of water he kept hidden in a corner of the room. "I'm going to make sure I'm so busy that Mr. Lloyd will tell Mr. Gore that he's crazy if he thinks I'm going to be sent to the fields," he said.

For the rest of the morning, Frederick cleaned everything he could find several times. He made sure that he didn't stop even for a minute. Once, Lucretia told him she had never seen him work so fast and asked him if there was something wrong.

"No, ma'am, Mrs. Lucretia," Frederick replied without stopping. "I just want to make sure that I always do my work the best I can."

"Oh, you don't have anything to worry about, Frederick," Lucretia said. "You're the hardest-working boy I've ever had. But I want you to slow down so you don't drop dead from exhaustion."

"Yes, ma'am," Frederick said. He only slowed down a little bit, though, and mainly because he was having difficulty catching his breath. Still, he worked at a faster pace than he ever had before.

Once, when he was waxing the banisters of the stairs that led to the second floor of the Great House, Mr. Lloyd and Mr. Gore came down, and Mr. Gore said, "Look at that boy go! He's faster than a whirling dervish."

"That's Lucretia's boy," Mr. Lloyd said as they continued on down the steps. "She wouldn't get rid of him for anything."

When the two men disappeared through a downstairs door, Frederick stopped for a moment to rest, then he resumed the waxing, but at a normal pace, now that he had heard what Mr. Lloyd had said about him.

Frederick felt himself slowly relaxing over the next week, now that he had decided that Mr. Gore wouldn't take him to work in the fields.

44

Still, he planned to make sure he stayed as far away from the new overseer as possible. So when Isaac told him that Lucretia wanted him to go to the woods to look for mushrooms, he was glad to be by himself.

Frederick took a cloth bag and a sharpened stick he used to dig the mushrooms out of the ground and headed to the woods. When he reached the tree line and thought no one could see him, he stopped and leaned up against one of the larger trees. Just being here, behind this tree, out of sight of everyone on the plantation, made him feel free, and he liked the idea. It was hard for him to understand those feelings sometimes.

A few feet away, a noise suddenly startled Frederick. His heart started to pound. *Someone followed me*, he thought, *and now I'm going to be punished for stopping*.

The noise got louder until Frederick was sure it was someone running through the undergrowth.

"You'd better stop, Demby!" a voice shouted in the distance. "You'd better stop now, or you're going to be in even more trouble!"

*Demby*, Frederick thought. *I've heard that name before*. He quickly crawled under a brush so he would be hidden but could still see what was happening.

Just then, a slave appeared in the small clearing, and Frederick could see the fear in the man's eyes. He hurriedly looked around, then ran for the thick underbrush on the other side. Within seconds, a white man appeared in the clearing, and Frederick gasped. It was Austin Gore.

"Demby, where are you?" Gore shouted. Frederick could see that he had a grin on his face. "You're being a bad slave, Demby, and I'm going to punish you when I find you."

"You going to have to come and get me, Mr. Austin," a voice shouted from beyond the undergrowth.

Frederick saw Gore's face flush with anger.

Gore withdrew a gun and started walking toward the underbrush. "Well, that's what I'm going to do, Demby," he said.

The only thing Frederick could think of now was that he had to help Demby in some way. He wasn't quite sure how, but he knew he couldn't live with himself if he just stayed where he was, like some coward. As quietly as he could, he crawled out from his hiding place, all the time keeping an eye on Gore's back. As soon as Gore plunged into the underbrush, Frederick stood up and ran to its edge.

Gore was making so much noise that Frederick knew any sound he made would be covered by Gore's, but he hadn't counted on Gore's stopping so suddenly, and he almost butted his head against the back of the overseer's legs.

Why did he stop? Frederick wondered.

It didn't take long to find out. Demby was in the middle of the creek, with water up to his waist. He must have known that Gore wouldn't come into the water after him.

"What's the matter, Mr. Austin?" Demby called. "Here I am. Come get me. You're not afraid of the water, are you?"

"I'm not afraid of anything, Demby, but I'm not going to get my clothes wet for a lowly slave," Gore said. "I'll just sit here and bide my time while you think about what's going to happen to you when you get out."

"Who said I was coming out, Mr. Austin?" Demby called.

Gore snorted but said nothing.

Frederick remained motionless, fearing that even if he breathed too loudly, Gore would hear him, but a sudden gust of wind caused the bushes to sway, making enough noise so that Frederick could move far enough away to stay hidden from Gore but still see what was happening.

The wind didn't let up, and from his hiding place, Frederick could see that Demby was shivering. He wondered how much longer the slave could stay where he was. He had also begun to think about what was going to happen to him if he came home without any mushrooms.

Demby shouted, "If I give myself up, Mr. Austin, what are you going to do to me?"

"I can't do too much, Demby," Gore said. "You're such a valuable slave to Captain Anthony, he'd be upset with me if I damaged you."

Frederick could see Demby's Adam's apple bobbing up and down as he swallowed hard. He was probably thinking what he should do, Frederick decided. Finally, he started walking slowly toward the bank. When he reached it, he climbed out and stood dripping in front of Gore.

Frederick heard the gun fire and he screamed. Without even thinking, he plunged through the bushes, into the clearing, and raced out of the woods. Only when he reached the garden did he slow down.

At the house, he found Isaac and told him what had happened.

"Oh, my Lord, son, you're in trouble now, if that Mr. Gore saw you," Isaac said.

"I don't think he saw me, or, if he did, he only saw the back of me," Frederick said, "and I don't think he can identify me that way."

"Where are the mushrooms?" Isaac asked.

"I didn't get any," Frederick replied.

Frederick was prepared for the worst to happen to him. While he was cleaning himself up, he decided to tell Lucretia that wild animals must have trampled the mushrooms earlier and that he hadn't seen any that were fit to eat.

Right before he got to Lucretia's sitting room, though, he heard voices coming from Captain Anthony's study. He crept closer and pretended to dust the furniture near the door.

"Of course you won't be put on trial for the

murder of a slave, Gore," Mr. Lloyd was saying. "Slaves aren't people, they're property."

"Still, Gore, Demby was one of my best men. You need to control your anger more," Captain Anthony said. "This may be the first one you've killed, but this isn't the first one you've damaged so much, they haven't been able to work for weeks, and that puts us behind."

"I'm sorry, sir," Mr. Gore said.

"Well, I'm sure we can settle this, Mr. Gore, if you'll agree to pay me the man's worth," Mr. Lloyd said. "I'll write down a figure and hand it to you and then you can tell me if you agree."

Frederick heard the scratching of a quill pen; then, after a few minutes, Mr. Gore said, "Yes, sir, that's a fair sum, I think."

"Yes, sir," Frederick said.

From the shuffling sounds the men were making, Frederick knew their meeting was over and that they would soon be leaving the room. He hurriedly made his way through several corridors until he had reached the back of the house. He was just about to enter the small room where he slept when someone grabbed his arm.

It was Isaac. "Where have you been?" he demanded.

"I wanted to find out what Mr. Gore's punishment was for killing Demby," Frederick said.

"And did you?" Isaac asked.

Frederick nodded. "He's just going to pay Colonel Lloyd some money, and nothing's going to happen to him."

"Of course not," Isaac said. "Now, I've righted things with Mrs. Lucretia about the mushrooms, and she understands, but you can't let this happen again, Frederick."

But Frederick wasn't listening. *One of these days*, he thought, *I'm going to leave this place, and I'm going to be free*.

# Young Barney and Old Barney

"Are you sure you're eight?" Young Barney asked Frederick one morning in the spring of 1826.

"I'm almost sure," Frederick replied. "If I'm not, I will be soon."

Young Barney expanded his nostrils as he took a deep breath, and then he twisted his lips, a habit Frederick found irritating. He didn't say anything, though. Young Barney and his father, Old Barney, took care of all of Colonel Lloyd's horses, and it was a job that Frederick wished he had. He had been hoping for weeks to convince Young Barney to let him work in the stables after he had finished his other chores.

There was something about the horses that made Frederick feel free. As they roamed the huge pasture lands, prancing and dancing, they seemed to challenge the notion that they belonged to anyone.

"Well, all right, then, if you're almost sure, because I could use the help," Young Barney said, "but you can't tell anybody, because I'll get into trouble."

"I won't tell," Frederick said.

"Even if Mrs. Lucretia asks you where you were?" Young Barney said.

Frederick nodded. "But she won't ask me. She trusts me, and she knows that I always do my work," he said. "Anyway, she's spending a week with a family down in Washington, so she's not here to say anything, and Isaac told me it was all right, just as long as I do my other chores."

Young Barney shook his head. "White folks are sure funny, I can tell you that," he said. "They're either very mean or very nice, and there aren't many of them who are very nice, but I can tell you for sure, there aren't any who are in between."

"That's the truth," Frederick said. He looked around. "Where's Old Barney?"

"He's in the barn, getting the grain ready," Young Barney said. "He's not moving around very fast this morning."

Frederick didn't even have to ask Young Barney why. He knew. He was sure that Colonel Lloyd had taken the whip to Old Barney the day before.

"Well, come on, we've got a lot of work to do," Young Barney said.

Frederick followed Young Barney to the stables where some of Colonel Lloyd's prize stallions were in their stalls, ready to be fed and groomed. Once inside, Frederick inhaled deeply. He never tired of what he called the "horse smell." It was a combination of hay and manure and horse sweat, and there was nothing unpleasant about it. In fact, Frederick had decided that it was one of the most wonderful smells in the world.

"You take General first," Young Barney said, "and I'll take Caesar."

"All right," Frederick said. General was a powerful black horse that Frederick had once seen throw Mr. Gore, which was one of the reasons he liked the animal so much.

When Frederick finished grooming General, he poured a bucket of feed in the trough, and General started eating. Frederick patted his neck, kissed it a couple of times, and then said, "I love you, General, and I hope I can always help take care of you."

Next to General's stall was Leonardo. Leonardo was a funny horse. He didn't seem to like many people, so he wasn't ridden as much, but that was exactly why Frederick liked him.

"Hello, Leonardo," Frederick whispered. "How are you today?"

Leonardo snorted and pawed at the hay that lay on the stall floor.

"Are you hungry?" Frederick whispered. "Well, let me brush you first, and then we'll—" Suddenly, he heard an angry voice at the door of the stable, and he ducked down so he couldn't be seen unless someone was peering directly into Leonardo's stall.

"All right, Old Barney, you lazy slave!" Colonel Lloyd shouted. "Where are you?"

For just a few seconds there was total silence in the stable, except for a snort from one of the horses at the other end. Frederick moved where he could peer through the boards of Leonardo's stall so he could see what was happening.

"Here I am, Colonel Lloyd," Old Barney said in a weak voice. He slowly appeared from the shadows in a far corner of the barn, and Frederick was stunned at what he saw.

Old Barney was hunched over, and the shirt he was wearing was in tatters, so that the red marks on his back from the beating he had been given the day before were easily visible.

"You come to me now, boy!" Colonel Lloyd shouted.

"Yes, sir, Colonel Lloyd," Old Barney said.

Suddenly, Young Barney appeared behind Old Barney and grabbed the back of his pants to stop him, but Old Barney managed to jerk loose and he continued walking slowly toward Colonel Lloyd. Frederick saw Young Barney disappear back into the shadows of the corner.

When Old Barney finally reached Colonel Lloyd, he bowed his head, as though he had the ritual memorized and knew exactly what to do.

"You're a lazy, good-for-nothing slave, Old Barney!" Colonel Lloyd shouted.

"Yes, sir, Colonel Lloyd," Old Barney said.

Frederick could see now that he had begun

to shake. For several more minutes, Colonel Lloyd continued to berate Old Barney, calling him every vile name Frederick had ever heard used with slaves, and even a few new ones. He told him that he knew nothing about how to take care of the horses and, calling the animals by name, said that Luther was lame and that George had his shoes on wrong and that General had sores where the saddle cinches had broken his flesh and gotten infected.

At that moment, Frederick knew that Colonel Lloyd was lying, because he had just finished brushing General and he knew that the horse didn't have sores anywhere on his body.

Finally, Colonel Lloyd said, "Down on your knees!"

Without saying a word, Old Barney removed his tattered shirt and dropped to his knees, his head still bowed. He knew what was coming.

Frederick held his breath for what seemed like an eternity, until Colonel Lloyd had finally finished and gone.

Within seconds, Young Barney had re-emerged from the shadows and run to his father.

Frederick jumped up, let himself out of Leonardo's stable, and joined him.

"Papa! Papa!" Young Barney was crying. "Let me help you up."

"Just leave me be, Young Barney," Old Barney said. "I just need to lie here a minute."

Young Barney turned his tear-stained face to Frederick and said, "We do the best we can. We love these horses, and we make sure that nothing happens to them. I don't understand why Colonel Lloyd is always able to find something wrong with them."

"There's nothing wrong with the horses," Frederick said. "Colonel Lloyd is making it all up."

"But, why?" Young Barney asked. "What else can we do?"

Frederick shook his head. "You can't do

anything else, Young Barney. It has nothing to do with the horses, really. Colonel Lloyd is a cruel man, and for some reason he enjoys hurting people. It'll never stop. It'll never stop until we're all free."

Always before, Frederick had prided himself on his work, keeping busy, doing the best job he could possibly do, thinking that would keep him safe. But after he witnessed Old Barney's whipping at the hands of Colonel Lloyd, he realized that he had no control over what could happen to him. With that knowledge, his whole world at the Great House changed.

Frederick knew now that any white person walking by who just happened to take a disliking to him could whip him, and he couldn't do anything about it. So when Lucretia told him that he was going to be sent to Baltimore to live with the Hugh Auld family, he was relieved. Even though Hugh was the brother of Lucretia's husband, Frederick hoped that maybe things would be better for him in Baltimore.

"Why are you so happy about leaving us?" Isaac asked.

"It can't be any worse than here, but it might be better," Frederick told him. "I've never been anywhere except around Great House Farm, and I'm looking forward to an adventure. I want to see the rest of the world."

"You won't be seeing the rest of the world, Frederick," Isaac told him. "You'll just be seeing Baltimore, and that's not really all that far from here."

"But I'll get to take a ship there, Isaac, and I won't have to walk," Frederick said.

"That's true, son, that's true," Isaac said. He put his arm around Frederick's shoulders. "Old Isaac's going to miss you, but you know I wish you well."

"I'm going to miss you, too, Isaac, very much," Frederick said. He pulled away and gave Isaac a big grin. "Guess what? Mrs. Lucretia said she was going to give me a pair of long pants, my first, if I'll clean up really nice. Will you help me?"

"You know I will, son," Isaac said. He gave Frederick a once-over. "We'll make you look right for Mr. Hugh Auld and his family and the rest of Baltimore."

"Thank you, Isaac," Frederick said.

"Well, you'd better go start that water boiling, Frederick," Isaac said, "because with as much dirt and dead skin as you have on you, this is going to take a whole day of hard scrubbing at least!"

Frederick grinned. "That's fine with me!" he said.

# Sailing to Baltimore

It was on a Saturday morning when Colonel Lloyd's ship, *Sally Lloyd*, headed down the Miles River toward Chesapeake Bay and Baltimore.

Frederick walked to the back of the sloop so he could give the plantation one final look. "I never want to see you again," he whispered. "I'll miss Isaac and Mrs. Lucretia, and I'll probably wonder what my brothers and sisters are doing, my grandmother, too, but I want to see the rest of the world. This is a new beginning for me."

Frederick didn't want to look backward all the way to Baltimore, though, so he walked to the front of the sloop again and spent the rest of the day looking ahead to his future.

In the afternoon, *Sally Lloyd* stopped at Annapolis, the capital of Maryland, but the sloop only stopped for a few minutes, so there was no time to go ashore.

"What do you think about Annapolis, Frederick?" Patrick, one of the black deck-hands, asked him.

"It's bigger than Great House Farm," Frederick said. "I never thought I'd see a town so large."

Patrick laughed. "If you think Annapolis is big, son, you won't believe Baltimore," he said. "It's a sight to see, I can tell you that."

When they arrived early Sunday morning at Smith's Wharf, Frederick saw that it was true, it was a sight to see. He hadn't been prepared for what lay before him.

Rich, another one of the hands belonging

to the sloop, came up and said, "I'm supposed to take you to your new home, Frederick, so we'd best be on our way."

"I'm ready," Frederick said.

Rich's legs were much longer than his, and it took a lot of effort for Frederick to keep up with him. They twisted and turned through so many cobblestoned streets that Frederick was soon so confused, he couldn't have found his way back to the sloop if he had had to. Rich seemed to know exactly where he was going, though, and Frederick decided that he must be very well acquainted with the city.

Finally, Rich said, "Well, this is Alliciana Street, Frederick, and Mr. and Mrs. Hugh Auld live in that redbrick house with the black shutters. This is going to be your new home."

For just a moment, Frederick thought he was surely dreaming and that any minute he'd awaken in his dark room back at Great House Farm. Isaac would be there, telling him to get up, that he had work to do, and that if he didn't watch out, he'd be sent to the fields.

When Rich started up the front stoop, Frederick held back. "Shouldn't we go around back?" he whispered.

Rich shook his head and knocked.

Within minutes, the front door opened, and there stood a man and a woman and a little boy.

"Mr. and Mrs. Auld and Master Thomas," Rich said, "I have brought Frederick to you."

Now, Frederick was sure that he had suddenly been taken up to heaven, because he had never seen a white face smiling at him with such kindness as that of Mrs. Auld's. She looked like an angel. Before Frederick could get a word out of his mouth, a white hand was reaching out to him and the woman was saying, "We are so glad you've come to live with us, Frederick. We hope you'll be happy here."

"Thank you, ma'am," Frederick finally managed to say. He turned to look at Rich, and Rich smiled at him.

• • •

Once inside the house, with the door closed, Frederick simply had no idea what to do next. Even though Mrs. Auld had his hand, Frederick stood frozen to a spot on the soft rug. But Mrs. Auld's soft voice made him relax, and Frederick followed her and Thomas into the kitchen.

Right away, Frederick smelled the wonderful aroma of baking bread, and his mouth started to water, but he willed it to stop because he knew that he would never taste it.

"Here, Frederick," Mrs. Auld said. "Sit in this chair, and I'll butter you some fresh bread and top it with jam."

Frederick couldn't believe his ears. He wanted to tell her that she shouldn't do that, that she would get in trouble, but then he realized that this was her house and that she could do as she pleased. With head bowed, he said, "Yes, ma'am," and took a seat in a sturdy, dark wooden chair.

Thomas climbed up on a chair opposite Frederick and stared at him. Frederick gave him a quick smile, and Thomas smiled back, but it scared Frederick so much, he bowed his head again.

"You're going to live with us," Thomas said. "You're going to be my friend."

Once again, Frederick gulped. "Yes," he said. "I'm going to live with you, and I'm going to be your friend."

He was sure that a rebuke from Mrs. Auld would come next. When it didn't, he glanced quickly in her direction and saw that she was spreading butter and jam on a slice of bread that she had cut from the loaf. She still had a smile on her face. Frederick was amazed.

"Now, then, Frederick," Mrs. Auld said as she placed the bread in front of him, "we'll let you eat while we talk about what you'll be doing for us."

"Yes, ma'am," Frederick said.

Frederick had never tasted anything like

the buttered bread and jam he had been given. It seemed to melt in his mouth. It was so good, it was hard to concentrate on what Mrs. Auld was telling him, but he did hear most of it, especially the part about her never having had a slave before, and that she didn't know exactly what she was supposed to do.

When Frederick finished his bread, he said, "Thank you, ma'am," but he kept his head down until Mrs. Auld said, "Why don't you look at me when you talk, Frederick? That's the polite thing to do."

"I'm sorry, ma'am," Frederick said. He could feel himself trembling, even though he didn't want to, but he didn't know any other way of acting around white people. "I'm sorry, ma'am," he repeated.

Mrs. Auld sighed. "Well, we won't worry about that now." She stood up. "This is the time I usually read to Thomas. You can help me, since one of your duties will be to take care of him." She turned to Thomas. "Are you ready for a story?"

"Yes, Mama," Thomas said.

Frederick followed Mrs. Auld and Thomas into a room that had walls lined with books.

"This is our library, Frederick," Mrs. Auld said. "I suspect that you and Thomas will be spending a lot of time in here."

Mrs. Auld went to one of the shelves, selected a book, and then sat down on a settee. Thomas climbed up into her lap. "You sit here next to us, Frederick," she said.

Frederick did as he was told, but he found himself scarcely able to breathe, being this close to a white person.

"I know that you're eight, Frederick," Mrs. Auld said, "so you must know how to read pretty well by now. Why don't you start?"

"Ma'am?" Frederick said. He was sure he hadn't heard her correctly. "Did you say you wanted *me* to read?"

"Yes," Mrs. Auld said. "You'll be reading a lot

to Thomas, so we might as well get started."

"I'm sorry, ma'am, but I don't know how to read," Frederick said.

Mrs. Auld blinked. "You don't know how to *read*?" she asked incredulously. "Well, what did they teach you at school?"

"I've never been to school," Frederick said. "I've just been working at Great House Farm."

Frederick could see in Mrs. Auld's eyes that she was genuinely astonished at what he had just told her.

Finally, Mrs. Auld said, "Well, Frederick, if you're going to live in this house, then you're going to learn how to read, and I'm going to teach you."

Now, it was Frederick's turn to be astonished.

Mrs. Auld was true to her word. Every day, when Frederick had finished his chores, he would accompany Mrs. Auld to the library,

where she taught him the letters of the alphabet.

"Oh, my, you're a fast learner, Frederick," Mrs. Auld said after the first week. "This is wonderful."

When Frederick had mastered the alphabet Mrs. Auld began teaching him short words.

"If you know the letters of the alphabet, Frederick, the next step is putting those letters together to form words," Mrs. Auld said.

One morning, several weeks later, Frederick awakened early, even more excited about finishing his chores, so he could start his lessons. Today, Mrs. Auld was going to let him read a passage from the Bible. Frederick had been practicing because he wanted to make sure he read perfectly, but the minute he got to the kitchen to feed Thomas his breakfast, he knew something was wrong.

Mr. Auld was still seated at the table, which surprised Frederick, because he usually left early. Mrs. Auld was across from him, her head bowed.

"I'm glad you're here, Frederick," Mr. Auld said. "I've learned something quite disturbing."

Frederick swallowed hard and felt his heart start to pound. He couldn't imagine what he could have done wrong, but all of a sudden, he pictured himself being put back on *Sally Lloyd* and returned to Great House Farm. He bowed his head and waited to find out what it was.

"My wife has been teaching you how to read," Mr. Auld said. "I've told her to stop at once. Educated slaves are unmanageable and worthless, and I can't have that."

Frederick was stunned. He was almost relieved that it wasn't something so horrible that he would have to leave, but he was also greatly disappointed. "Yes, sir, Mr. Auld, I understand, sir," he said.

"I knew you'd see it that way, Frederick,

because I could tell from the moment you arrived that you wanted to be a good slave," Mr. Auld said, "and good slaves always do exactly what the master wants."

"Yes, sir, Mr. Auld," Frederick said.

Frederick remained standing where he was, with his head bowed, until Mr. Auld had finished his breakfast, and then, once Mr. Auld had left, he sat down and fed Thomas.

For the rest of the day, Frederick busied himself with his chores. Several times he noticed that Mrs. Auld didn't look at him when she spoke. For that, Frederick was heartbroken. He made himself a promise before he went to sleep that night. Since Mrs. Auld was no longer allowed to teach him how to read, he would find another way to learn. He had decided that knowing how to read would be his way out of slavery.

# Learning to Read

When Frederick awakened the next morning, he looked through the tiny window in his room and saw Robert Worthington, a boy who lived nearby, on his way to fetch milk for his family. Even though Robert was white, he sometimes talked to Frederick about the things he was learning in school.

Suddenly, Frederick had an idea. *I'll fool you yet*, Mr. Auld, he thought. *I'll ask Robert to teach me how to read!*

Later that morning, Frederick found Mrs.

Auld in the library, writing a letter. "I'm finished with my morning chores, ma'am," he said. "I can go to the butcher's for the cook now."

"All right, Frederick, but don't tarry," Mrs. Auld said.

"Yes, ma'am," Frederick said.

The cook gave Frederick the coins he would need to pay for the meat. "If that isn't enough, then tell Master John that Mrs. Auld will settle the account later," she said.

Frederick started toward the front door, but the cook stopped him. "Use the rear entrance, Frederick," she said. When Frederick started to question her, she shook her head, and he knew that she had been ordered by the Aulds to tell him that.

Frederick took a deep breath and started toward the butcher shop. He was almost there when he saw Robert coming toward him, pulling his cart with the milk barrel on it. Frederick was disappointed to see that another neighborhood boy was with him now. The boy's name was James, and he was the skinniest white person Frederick had ever seen. Some of the slave children at Great House Farm were skinnier, but that was because they never had enough to eat. Frederick didn't know why James was that way.

Frederick waved, and Robert waved back.

When the three boys reached one another, Robert and James stopped.

"Where you going?" Robert asked.

"To the butcher's," Frederick replied.

"Oh," Robert said. He shifted back and forth on his feet. "I've got milk here."

Frederick nodded. He had forgotten how slow Robert seemed sometimes. Now, he wondered if Robert would really be the right person to teach him how to read. Still, he needed to begin somewhere, so he said, "I want to learn how to read, Robert. Will you teach me?"

Robert blinked. "Why do you need to know how to read?" he asked. "My daddy says slaves don't need to know how."

"I just want to, that's all," Frederick said. "I'd like to know what words say."

"I can teach you," James said. "I know how to read better than Robert."

Frederick quickly looked back at Robert, wondering how he would react, but Robert merely said, "He's right, Frederick."

For Frederick, this was an unexpected turn of events. "Would you really do that?" he asked.

James nodded. "But you'd have to pay me," he said.

"I don't have any money," Frederick said.

"I can't do it for free," James said.

Suddenly, Frederick had an idea. "I can pay you in food," he said. "I've heard Mrs. Auld say that we have the best cook in Baltimore."

Frederick was astonished at how James's eyes lit up.

"I'll do it for food," James said.

Frederick held out his hand for James to shake, much like he had seen white men do when they were sealing business deals with each other. James looked puzzled for a minute, but then he took Frederick's hand and shook it. To Frederick it seemed as though he were shaking hands with a skeleton.

The lessons started the next day. Frederick had found a book in the library that he knew Mrs. Auld read from time to time. She seemed to enjoy it, so he decided this was the one James should use to teach him how to read.

*"Plays by William Shakespeare?"* James said when Frederick showed him the book. "Why do you want to read this?"

Frederick explained to him why he had chosen the book.

"Well, all right, but I don't know what good it'll do you if you're not going to be an actor,"

James said. He looked at the tied-up bundle in Frederick's hand. "Is that my food?" he asked.

"Yes," Frederick said. "It's fried chicken and a potato and a slice of buttered bread."

"There's a garden not far from here, where we can sit under a tree," James said. "No one will bother us. I go there all the time."

It didn't take James long to eat the food that Frederick had brought. After he had finished, James opened the book to the first page and showed Frederick the first sentence of the play *Julius Caesar*. "Hence! Home, you idle creatures, get you home: Is this a holiday?"

Frederick looked up at James in amazement. For some reason, this sounded very much like complaints he had heard at Great House Farm. Now he wasn't sure he had chosen the right book, but he repeated the words, anyway, as James pointed to them, and within the next few minutes he was able to look at words James pointed to randomly and pronounce them.

"That's good," James finally said. He stood up. "That shows me that you haven't just memorized the lines. You can actually recognize the words."

Frederick couldn't have been happier. "Can I meet you here tomorrow?" he asked.

James nodded. "But bring food," he said.

"I shall," Frederick told him.

As he started to leave, James added, "I'll choose the book this time."

When Frederick got home, the cook told him that Mrs. Auld was waiting for him in the library. He went directly there. He was still holding the book he had taken.

"Yes, ma'am?" Frederick said.

Mrs. Auld didn't look at him. She kept her eyes on the book in her hands. "I wondered what had happened to my volume of Shakespeare plays," she said. Now, she lifted her eyes so that they bore into Frederick. "Why did you steal my book, Frederick?" she asked.

"I didn't steal it, Mrs. Auld, ma'am, honestly," Frederick said. "I just wanted to read it."

"You are not to read anything in this house, Frederick!" Mrs. Auld shouted at him. She stood up, and Frederick saw that she was shaking from anger. It frightened him. "Do you understand me?"

"Yes, ma'am," Frederick said. He bowed his head.

"Look at me, Frederick!" Mrs. Auld shouted.

Frederick lifted his eyes. "Yes, ma'am," he repeated.

Frederick continued to stare at her until Mrs. Auld took a deep breath, which flared her nostrils, and turned away from him to look out the window of the parlor. Almost instantly, it seemed to him, her face seemed like the face of every slave owner he had ever seen. But Frederick didn't feel anger. Only sadness.

"You may leave now, Frederick," Mrs. Auld

said, still not looking at him. "You have work to do."

The next day, when Frederick met James in the garden, he forgot all about the Aulds' books, because James brought a book called *The Columbian Orator.*

"It talks about the freeing of the slaves, Frederick," James said. "It belongs to the minister at our church." He grinned. "I told him I was teaching you to read for food."

Frederick was panicked. "Why did you do that?" he asked.

James touched his arm. "You don't have to worry about him, Frederick," he said. "He doesn't believe in slavery."

Frederick relaxed. "I want to read this book, James," he said.

James opened the book to the first page and started pronouncing each word. Frederick repeated them. Slowly, Frederick began to recognize certain words before James would say them. When James told Frederick that he was amazed at how fast he was able to read the book, Frederick said, "It's because I want to do this more than anything else in the world, and when you want something as bad as I want this, it becomes easier and easier."

As they progressed through the book, Frederick could feel a change coming over him. He knew without a doubt that he did not want to be a slave any longer. He came to see how unfair it was for white men to keep black men in bondage. But on the day they finished *The Columbian Orator*, Frederick looked at James and said, "I still don't know how I can become free."

James thought for a few minutes, then shrugged his shoulders and said, "I don't know, either, Frederick."

The next day, when Frederick went for his reading lesson, James wasn't there. He waited as long as he thought he could, then he stood up to leave, but in the distance, he saw James running toward him.

"Frederick!" James shouted. "Wait!"

When James reached him, Frederick said, "I thought you weren't coming. I thought you didn't want to teach me anymore."

"It's not that, Frederick. We're moving," James said. "My father is going to be an overseer at a plantation in Virginia."

At the mention of the words "plantation" and "overseer," Frederick felt a chill go through him. "When?" he asked. James was a good teacher, and he couldn't imagine learning from anyone else. "Can't you stay here?" Frederick knew it was a silly question the moment it came out his mouth.

James shook his head. "I wish I could," he said. "I like Baltimore, and . . ." He hesitated. "And I like having you as a friend."

Frederick wasn't sure that was true, but he grabbed James's hand and shook it. "Thank you for teaching me," he said.

"Thank you for giving me food," James said. "Papa said we'd have more food on the plantation. That's mainly why we're going."

Frederick watched James disappear back down the street. He didn't know what to do now. He felt lost. It was a Friday, and on Fridays, the Aulds let him wander around Baltimore, just to familiarize himself with the city so he'd know where to go on errands when they needed him to do so. That's what he decided to do now. After a couple of hours, though, he ended up at Baltimore's wharf because he enjoyed looking at the big ships tied up at the piers.

Frederick was glad to see that the wharf was busier than usual today. No one really seemed to mind when he wandered around, up, and down the moorings, looking at the activity around each ship, but when it was busy, he knew that people probably wouldn't even notice him.

Frederick walked past the first ship, then

leaned up against a pole by the second ship and watched as two men rolled barrels down the gangplank and then loaded them onto a wagon.

After a few minutes, one of the men shouted, "Laddy, would you like to give us a hand? We'll give you some coins for your help."

At first, Frederick wasn't sure if he had actually understood the man. He knew the man was speaking English, but he had never heard it spoken that way.

"You want *me* to help you?" Frederick said to the man.

"If you're of a mind to, Laddy," the man said. "For I've sprained me back, and it's starting to hurt in a bad way."

The man with the bad back introduced himself as Patrick. The other man's name was Corben. For the next two hours, Frederick rolled the barrels down the gangplank, sometimes by himself, sometimes helping Patrick with his. Finally, they were finished, and Patrick said, "You're a fine worker, Laddy." He reached into his pocket and pulled out two coins. "This is for your trouble."

Frederick was astonished. He was positive that these coins would buy meat for a week. "Thank you, sir," he said.

"You should think about coming to Ireland with us, if you're looking for work," Corben said. "We're taking a load back, and then we'll pick up another load for Baltimore."

"I can't do that," Frederick said.

"Why not?" Patrick asked. "You're a strong lad. You could handle the work."

"I'm a slave," Frederick said. "I belong to Mr. and Mrs. Auld."

Patrick spat. "That's terrible," he said. "You're too good to be a slave, Laddy."

"You should run away," Corben told him. "Haven't you ever heard of the Underground Railroad?"

Frederick shook his head. "I know about

trains that run aboveground, but not ones that run underground," he said.

The two men laughed.

"It's not a real train," Patrick said. "It's just a secret way for slaves to escape to some of the northern states or even to Canada."

"Can't you be free in Maryland?" Frederick asked.

Corben shook his head. "Maryland's a southern state," he said. "You need to go to someplace like New York or Massachusetts."

Suddenly, Frederick got excited at the thought of leaving Maryland to become a freeman, but almost as soon, he remembered stories he had heard about white men who tricked slaves into escaping so they could capture them and then collect a reward. Were Patrick and Corben like that? he wondered.

"I'll think about it," Frederick finally said. "Thank you for letting me work for you."

Both men held out their hands for Frederick to shake. He did.

As Frederick left the wharf area, he knew he would never forget what he had learned, but he also know that he had to make sure that the Aulds never found out about it.

# Frederick Becomes
# a Field Hand

By the end of 1831, Frederick, now thirteen, was reading very well, but he decided he also wanted to be able to write. He tried copying words from some of the books he was reading, but they never looked the way he wanted them to. Several times over the last few weeks he had had the opportunity to glance at letters Mrs. Auld was writing to her friends, and Frederick had decided that he wanted his words to look like hers.

When Frederick mentioned this to some

of the ship's carpenters at Baltimore's wharf, men he had learned to trust, they told him what he saw in books were the *printed* letters and what he saw in Mrs. Auld's letters were the *script* letters.

Then, one day, good fortune struck. While Frederick was cleaning Thomas's room, he moved aside some clothes and found bound pieces of paper in which Thomas himself had been practicing his written letters. Frederick knew this was exactly what he needed.

"What are you doing, Frederick?"

Frederick whirled around to see Thomas standing at the door to his room. "I'm cleaning, sir," he said.

"Well, be careful not to disturb my schoolwork," Thomas said, coming into the room. "I'm very particular about it."

"What exactly is it that you're doing here?" Frederick asked.

"What does it look like I'm doing?" Thomas said. "I'm practicing my letters. That's how we white people learn to write." He took a deep breath. "Of course, slaves wouldn't understand, because they don't need to write."

"Of course, Master Thomas," Frederick said.

From that day on, Frederick kept any discarded pieces of paper he could find and, when Thomas was out of the house and Mrs. Auld was either busy downstairs or gone, Frederick would practice writing his letters. In time, Frederick's handwriting was as good as—if not better than—Thomas's.

Early in 1832, Frederick's world seemed to fall apart. Captain Anthony died, and his property was to be divided between his two remaining children, Andrew and Lucretia. Since Frederick was still considered to be Captain Anthony's property, he was ordered to return to Great House Farm to be counted.

"I'm afraid," he told the Aulds' cook on the

morning of his departure. "Mrs. Lucretia was always very kind to me, but Mr. Andrew is an evil man."

"You'll survive, Frederick," the cook said to him. Then she did something she had never done before. She took him in her arms and held him for a few minutes. "I'll be praying for you, son," she whispered in his ear.

The voyage back to the Great House Plantation was much the same as the voyage to Baltimore. Captain Rowe steered the schooner *Wild Cat* expertly through Chesapeake Bay until they arrived at dockside at the place where Frederick was born.

As he leaned against the side of the ship, Frederick spotted a familiar face. Even though it had been almost five years, he immediately recognized his brother, Perry. Frederick waved and shouted, "Perry!"

Perry looked up and, recognizing Frederick, waved back. Almost immediately, Andrew

Anthony grabbed Perry by the shoulders and threw him to the ground.

"Stop it!" Frederick shouted.

Suddenly, someone grabbed him by the throat and pulled him away from the side of the ship.

"Do you want the same thing to happen to you?"

Frederick turned and was looking up into the face of one of the freeman deckhands.

"No," Frederick said.

"You're not in Baltimore anymore," the deckhand said. "You need to remember that."

As he leaned up against the foremast, Frederick realized that he was shaking, but it wasn't from fear. It was from a rage he felt inside.

"I can't live like this," Frederick whispered. "I *won't* live like this."

For a fleeting moment, Frederick tried to come up with a plan that would let him hide on the schooner and return with it to Baltimore, but he quickly decided that wouldn't work. Everyone knew that he was being returned to be counted like the rest of Captain Anthony's property. He knew that the schooner probably wouldn't be allowed to leave until he had been found.

As Frederick and the other passengers and crew disembarked, he scolded himself for wanting to escape before he had discovered how serious his brother's injuries were. He had just put one foot on the pier when he noticed that Perry was starting to stand up. He was paying so much attention to his brother that he didn't notice a drunken Andrew lurching toward him.

"You're mine now," Andrew said, slurring his words and grabbing Frederick's arm. "And if you try to use smart words with me, Frederick, I'll do to you what I just did to your brother."

Frederick felt himself losing control. He had just started to raise his right fist to punch

Andrew, when a voice in the crowd shouted, "Andrew!"

Frederick immediately recognized the voice. It belonged to Lucretia.

"Andrew! You come here right now!" Lucretia called. "You're needed at the Great House at once!"

Andrew let go of Frederick's arm and began lurching toward Lucretia. With her help, he got into a carriage, and they drove away together.

Frederick ran over to Perry.

"Welcome back, brother," Perry said.

"I wish I could say I was glad to be back," Frederick told him.

Two days later, at dawn, all the slaves were lined up with the pigs, the cattle, the goats, and the chickens so that Captain Anthony's property could be divided. Frederick, standing next to Perry, silently prayed that he'd be chosen by Lucretia, not by Andrew.

It was almost mid-morning when Lucretia and Andrew finally arrived, and Frederick could see easily that Andrew was drunk again.

The animals were divided first, then herded away into separate pens by men Andrew and Lucretia had chosen to be their overseers. Finally, only the slaves were left. Some of the younger children were crying.

"I wish I could do something to keep them quiet," Frederick whispered to Perry.

"They'll feel the sting of Andrew's whip if they don't stop," Perry whispered back.

After fewer than ten of the slaves had been divided into two groups, one for Andrew and one for Lucretia, Andrew whispered something to Lucretia, who nodded, then he returned to the carriage, and the driver headed back down the road for the Great House.

Frederick felt himself starting to relax. Even though it was still possible that he'd be given to Andrew, Andrew wouldn't be around for a while to lash out at anyone.

When Lucretia finally reached Frederick and Perry, she gave them both a big smile.

"I want you both," Lucretia said. "Perry, you'll stay here with me on the plantation."

"Yes, ma'am, Miss Lucretia," Perry said. He grinned at Frederick, then he took his place with the other slaves Lucretia had chosen.

"Frederick, I have heard very nice things from my husband's brother and his wife in Baltimore," Lucretia said. "I'm sending you back there so you can continue your good work."

Frederick couldn't believe what he had just heard. "Oh, thank you, ma'am," he said. "I won't do anything to anger you or the Aulds."

"I shouldn't expect less from you, Frederick," Lucretia said.

Two days later, Frederick was walking down the gangplank of the schooner *Wild Cat* in

Baltimore harbor. The instant his foot touched the dock, it was as though he had never left and the short time at Great House Farm had merely been a bad dream.

All of his thoughts about escaping to become a freeman came back to him, and he vowed to take up where he left off. Somehow, someway, he would escape, but until he figured out a perfect plan, he'd settle into his life in Baltimore. Robert wouldn't be here, he knew, but he was sure there was another white boy somewhere in the city who could be his teacher.

When Frederick finally arrived at the Aulds', he went to the backdoor and knocked so he wouldn't startle anyone by simply going inside. When the cook saw him, she gave him a big hug.

"Well, you are a sight for sore eyes," the cook said. "What are you doing back in Baltimore?"

Frederick told her what had happened.

106

Mrs. Auld came into the kitchen to see what was going on. For just a moment, when she saw Frederick, her eyes lit up, Frederick noticed, but then the light went out, and she became a slave owner.

Frederick handed her a letter. "This is from Mrs. Lucretia, ma'am," he said. "It explains why I'm back in Baltimore."

For Frederick, the next few hours were amazing. Almost immediately, Mrs. Auld gave him a list of errands to run, and he set about doing them. No one knew that he had been gone for several days, had stood in line with farm animals to be counted, and then had the good fortune to return to Baltimore.

Each day, after Frederick finished his errands, he would go to Baltimore harbor to watch the ships. He looked for Corben and Patrick, but he never saw them. He wanted to talk to them some more about the Underground Railroad. It was still hard for him to trust any white man right away, but he trusted them. If he didn't see them again for a while, though, he decided, he might take a chance on talking to some of the other workers on the wharf to see if any of them knew about the Underground Railroad.

As Frederick headed home, he began making plans for the next day. He would select a book from the library, one up high that wouldn't be missed, then while he was doing his errands tomorrow, he would read as many pages as he could, perhaps even practice writing some of the letters, and then he would go back to Baltimore harbor and find someone to talk to about the Underground Railroad.

Later, Frederick would remember that as soon as he entered the Aulds' house, he could feel that something was wrong, something that would cause him great grief for a long time before he came up with a final plan to escape slavery. He saw the cook standing at the stove. Normally, she would have turned around to greet him, but she kept her back to him.

Frederick had just opened his mouth to ask her what was wrong when Mr. Auld appeared at the door.

"Where have you been?" Mr. Auld demanded.

"I've been doing my errands, sir," Frederick replied. Almost at once, he felt himself starting to tremble. "Is anything wrong?"

"Don't you dare question me, Frederick," Mr. Auld said. "You need to pack your things at once."

Frederick was dumbfounded. "Why, sir?" he asked.

Mr. Auld slapped him hard. "Did you not understand when I told you not to question me?" he said.

Frederick bowed his head. "I understand, sir," he managed to say. "I'm sorry, sir."

"Mrs. Lucretia has died, and my brother Thomas is to be remarried to Miss Rowena

Hamilton," Mr. Auld said. "Early tomorrow morning you'll take the sloop *Amanda* to St. Michaels, Maryland. You are now my brother's property, and you will be living on the plantation there."

"Yes, sir, Mr. Auld," Frederick said.

The cook managed to give Frederick his dinner before Mr. Auld locked him inside his room. At first, Frederick couldn't comprehend why this had been done, but when his mind finally cleared, he realized that it was to keep him from trying to run away.

*I should have listened to Patrick and Corben*, Frederick thought, as he lay on his pallet, waiting for morning to come. *From that first day, I should have trusted them to help me. If I had, I'd be a freeman now, not heading toward St. Michaels, with no idea of what kind of life I'll have there.*

Frederick managed to get a few hours of sleep before Mr. Auld opened his door and told him that they were leaving at once. A carriage was waiting in front of the house. As Frederick walked toward it, he thought it might be possible to jump off somewhere along the way, then hide until he could talk to someone at the docks who might help him escape. Unfortunately, Mr. Auld had probably thought about the same thing, for he tied Frederick to a bar and gave the driver instructions not to untie him until he had reached the docks.

The *Amanda* was ready to sail when Frederick arrived, so there was no chance to escape then, either. Once aboard, Frederick was locked inside a small cabin. He knew that Mr. Auld had probably instructed the captain to make sure Frederick didn't jump overboard and try to swim to shore. But Frederick did not know how to swim.

When fifteen-year-old Frederick arrived at St. Michaels, he was taken to the slave quarters, a row of windowless shacks behind a grove of trees, out of sight of the main house. He only had time to deposit his meager belongings on a dirty quilt in one corner when one of the house slaves, Amos, took him to the main house and told him to wash all of the floors.

"I don't know how," Frederick told the man. "I've never done it before."

"You'd better learn fast, then," the man said. "You get down on your knees and you scrub and scrub and then you scrub some more. The mistress likes to see her face in the shine," he added. "She—" Amos suddenly stopped talking and bowed his head.

Slowly, Frederick turned around. Thomas Auld was standing in the doorway, looking at him. He had a whip in his hand. "Frederick," he said. "I see you're finally back."

"Yes, sir," Frederick said.

"Come here," Mr. Auld said.

Frederick did as he was told.

"Kneel," Mr. Auld said.

Frederick knelt, and Thomas Auld lashed his back.

When Auld saw the tears streaming down Frederick's face, he said, "There will be more of those, you can be sure, for I have been counting the days until I could punish you for fooling my late wife into thinking you were worth more than you are."

"Yes, sir, Master Auld," Frederick said.

Thomas Auld wheeled around and left the room. When Frederick turned to look back at Amos, the man was no longer in the room. He was alone with a bucket of soapy water and a rough cloth.

Nothing Frederick did pleased Thomas Auld or his wife. He was whipped every day. If he got back late to the room he shared with ten other slaves, the food that had been set in a corner on the floor was gone. Frederick either had to beg or steal food to keep from starving to death. Even when he managed to eat, the food was usually rotten, something that most animals would have turned up their nose at.

Finally, one evening, just as Frederick had started back toward the house, Thomas Auld blocked his way on the path. Frederick prepared himself to be whipped, but instead, Auld said, "I'm sending you to a slave breaker, boy."

With his head bowed, Frederick said, "Yes, sir."

"Do you know what a slave breaker is, Frederick?" Auld demanded.

Frederick shook his head. "No, sir," he said.

"Slave breakers make you more manageable," Auld said.

"Yes, sir," Frederick said.

With that, Auld turned and stalked off. When the man was out of sight, Frederick actually managed a smile. "Thank you, Mr. Auld," he said to the wind. "Nothing could be worse than living with you."

# The Slave Breaker

On a bitterly cold January morning in 1834, Frederick left St. Michaels for Edward Covey's farm near Chesapeake Bay, seven miles away. He was wearing the clothes he had arrived in, almost a year earlier. Now, they were mostly threads and couldn't keep the strong winds from chilling him to the bone.

Along the road, Frederick passed by fields he had worked in just a few months earlier, now covered with patches of snow, but with the dead stalks of whatever had been planted in them and then harvested still visible in places.

The closer Frederick got to Chesapeake Bay, the fiercer and more biting the winds were. After a while, he no longer had much feeling in his hands or feet. He was sure that if he didn't get to Covey's farm soon, he would freeze to death. Finally, Frederick saw a weathered wooden sign nailed to a fence post, which had the name COVEY on it, and he knew this was the end of his journey.

Covey's house was certainly larger than the houses the slaves lived in at St. Michaels, but the outside of it looked about the same, with its unpainted and weathered wood. Frederick tried to knock, but with the first strike of his fist against the door he recoiled in pain and instead had to use his elbow. Even that wasn't much better, but it must have been heard inside, for within a couple of minutes, a wrinkled old white woman opened the door.

116

"Are you the slave from St. Michaels?" she asked.

"Yes, ma'am." Frederick nodded.

"I'm Mrs. Covey," the woman said. "Go around back, and my husband will be out shortly."

Frederick did as he was told, but "shortly" turned out to be longer than he thought it would, and by the time Mr. Covey appeared, Frederick could hardly move.

"I need you to take the oxcart and fill it up with wood," Covey told Frederick.

"Could I warm myself up and have something to eat first?" Frederick asked.

Covey blinked and looked as if he had been punched in the face. "Where do you think you are, boy, and *what* do you think you are?" he demanded.

"I know what I am, Mr. Covey, and I know where I am, too," Frederick said, "but I've walked a long way, sir, and I'm hungry."

Covey studied Frederick's face for a few

117

minutes, then a crooked smile slowly appeared on his face, and he started nodding his head. "Mr. Auld was right," he said. "You're too spirited to be a good slave." The smile suddenly disappeared. "That's what people pay me for, boy, to break you of that, so you just do what I told you to do, if you know what's good for you."

"Yes, sir, Mr. Covey," Frederick said. He looked around. "Where is the oxcart?"

"It's in the barn over there," Covey said. "Now, hurry up. My wife is late preparing supper because you tarried too long between here and St. Michaels, and there's no wood in the house."

Frederick started toward the barn.

"No matter what happens, boy, don't you let go of the rope that's tied to the horns of the lead ox," Mr. Covey shouted at him. "Those animals cost me a lot of money, and I won't have some slave ruin them."

"Yes, sir, Mr. Covey!" Frederick shouted back.

Frederick had seen oxen before, but only from a distance, on the roads as they passed by the St. Michaels plantation, so when he opened the barn door and went inside, he was absolutely astonished at the size of the animals. He stood for just a moment, in amazement at how strong they looked. All of a sudden, he remembered hearing his grandmother say that certain men on the plantation were as strong as an ox, and that was the only reason they were able to survive the hard work.

Just as Frederick untied the rope from a pole, the lead ox snorted, scaring him to death and causing him to drop the rope on the ground. Frederick was sure that both oxen were sizing him up, but he knew he had to do what Mr. Covey said or he'd be in serious trouble. Slowly, he bent down and picked up the end of the rope. He could feel the animals' eyes following him as he did. He managed to wrap the rope around his wrist and then clutch the end of it tightly in the palm of his hand.

"All right, you two," Frederick said, "we have an errand to do, and I expect you to help me do it."

The oxen ignored him.

"Let's go," Frederick said. He gently tugged on the rope, but nothing happened. "You heard me!" he said. "Come on!" This time, he tugged a little harder, and the oxen moved a few inches, then stopped, and then started again, with the wheels of the cart making a loud creaking sound.

Frederick and the oxen made it to the barn door, but a blast of wind immediately sliced through him, and his eyes began to water. Still, he continued to pull at the rope, and the oxen followed. Ahead, Frederick could see the tree line at the back of a pasture, so they headed in that direction. Now, Frederick's eyes were watering so much from their exposure to the cold wind that the trees seemed like a blurry brown. Finally, they began to come into focus as he

120

got closer to them, and Frederick started to relax.

Suddenly, a loud squawking filled the air, and Frederick felt the oxen jerk back, nearly pulling his hand from his arm. "Halt!" he shouted.

Instead of obeying Frederick, the oxen plunged into the trees, dragging him along with them.

"Stop! Stop!" Frederick cried.

The oxen only raced deeper into the woods. Frederick could feel the roughage on the ground tearing his chest. Desperately, he tried to let go of the rope, but it had become tangled in such a way that it was bound to his wrist. And he knew that if he lost the oxen and the cart, he would pay for it with a way that would be much worse than anything that was happening to him now, so he decided to hold on.

Suddenly, there was a crashing sound. For just a moment, Frederick saw the cart in the air above him, and then it landed upside down on top of him.

Frederick was amazed that he was still alive. He slowly untangled himself from the rope and crawled through the side of the cart. When he stood up, he realized that the thick underbrush had stopped the runaway oxen.

"I don't think the cart is broken," Frederick said to them. "We're lucky."

The oxen just looked at him.

It took all of his strength, but Frederick finally managed to right the cart and retie the rope to the horns of the lead ox.

As he surveyed the area around him, Frederick realized that he could probably fill most of the cart with the twigs and dead branches, all within a few feet of him, so he decided the experience would have a positive ending after all.

"Maybe you were just taking me here," Frederick said to the oxen. "Thank you."

Frederick worked steadily for about an

hour, filling the cart with wood he thought would burn well. The thick underbrush broke the cold wind, so only seldom did he feel a chill. When he finally finished, having stacked every piece of wood as close together as he could and filled in almost every space with twigs and smaller branches, he stood back and admired his work.

"This should make Mr. Covey happy," he said. "He'll have enough firewood to last him for a while."

Frederick finally managed to turn the oxen and the cart around so they were headed back in the direction of Mr. Covey's house. He was sure that this trip wouldn't be as difficult. He couldn't imagine the oxen running away from him with such a heavy load.

Just as they reached the edge of the woods, though, squawking birds once again caused the oxen to bolt. As before, they dragged Frederick on the ground beside them. He just barely managed to stay clear of their pounding hooves.

Up ahead, Frederick could see a fence, and he was sure that it would stop the oxen. Instead, they plowed through it, breaking several of the posts, before they came to a halt.

Frederick lay on the ground, trying to catch his breath. He had just started to get up when he felt someone grab the collar of his shirt and pull him up the rest of the way. Now, he was looking into the angry face of Mr. Covey.

"What'd I tell you?" Covey demanded.

"It wasn't my fault, sir," Frederick said. "They just—"

But Covey didn't let him finish.

The next morning, Frederick could hardly move, but he threw back the rough blanket and managed to stand up. There were red marks from the whip all over him. What was left of his clothes were in a pile beside the blanket. It took a lot of effort for him to put them on.

Once dressed, Frederick walked slowly toward the backdoor of Covey's house. When he reached it, he knocked. It was finally answered by Mrs. Covey, but she only showed half of her face.

"What do you want?" she demanded.

"I want to know what Mr. Covey wants me to do today, ma'am," Frederick said.

"Mr. Covey went into the village," Mrs. Covey said. "He'll be gone most of the day."

"Thank you, ma'am," Frederick said.

Frederick went to the barn and climbed up into the loft. From there, he could see the ships in Chesapeake Bay, and it gave him peace. He stayed there until nightfall.

For the next six months, Frederick's life was the same, day in and day out. He'd awaken, go to Mr. Covey's backdoor to find out what he was to do that day, then he'd do it to the best of his ability, which was never good enough, and then Mr. Covey would whip him. Each day, Frederick vowed that he wouldn't be broken, but slowly, he knew that if he stayed much longer, he wouldn't be able to hold up to the punishment.

One spring morning, when Frederick awakened, he felt as though he were on fire. He couldn't get up. He tried several times, but each time, his body refused to obey his command. Finally, he collapsed back onto the old blanket and lay still, praying that Mr. Covey would not miss him. He knew it was foolish even hoping it, but still, Frederick couldn't move.

"Ah, Frederick, I couldn't imagine where you might have gone," Mr. Covey said from the door of the shack. "For a minute, I thought you had run away, but if there's one thing you're not, it's stupid."

"I'm sick, Mr. Covey," Frederick managed to say. "I can't move."

"No, you're way too smart to do something like that," Mr. Covey continued, oblivious to what Frederick had just told him. "But that's the problem, isn't it?"

The sun was behind Mr. Covey, so all Frederick saw was a silhouette approaching him, but this silhouette had a whip in his hands.

When the first blow struck, Frederick was amazed to find that he didn't feel a thing.

Finally, Covey stopped, but he left with a final warning. "I'm going back to the field now, Frederick, and you'd better be there in fifteen minutes, or I'll kill you."

Frederick knew that with Covey, this was no idle threat. There was no way he could stay here any longer, he decided. Somehow, someway, he had to make it back to Thomas Auld's house. *Surely, if I tell him Mr. Covey is going to kill me, he'll let me stay there*, he thought. *After all, what good will I be to him if I'm dead?*

Frederick struggled to sit, then stand up, and finally he managed to make it to the door. It was seven miles back to St. Michaels. He had no choice but to use what strength he had left to take him there.

# No One Will Ever Whip Me Again!

It was dark when Frederick finally reached the Aulds' house. He knew he wasn't supposed to enter from the front, but he was sure he couldn't go any farther. As it was, once he had the Aulds' house in sight, he had fallen to his knees and had slowly dragged himself along the dirt road to the porch. Pulling himself up the steps to the door seemed to take forever. In fact, he was sure that his faint knocks probably wouldn't be heard by anyone, but Mrs. Auld just happened to be passing through the parlor and thought she heard a noise.

When she opened the front door, she screamed, "Thomas! There's a wild animal on the porch!"

"I'm not an animal, ma'am," Frederick managed to say. "It's Frederick. I've been at Mr. Covey's."

At that moment, Thomas Auld appeared beside his wife. He had a lantern in his hand. "What are you doing back here, boy?" he demanded. "Covey didn't tell me he was finished with you."

"I'm hurt, Mr. Auld." Frederick gasped. "I think I'm going to die."

"I'm going back to bed, Thomas," Mrs. Auld said. "My heart can't take much more of this."

Mr. Auld stepped out onto the porch and held the lantern above Frederick. "You're filthy, boy," he said. "You look as though you've been dragging yourself through the dirt."

"I have been, sir," Frederick said.

"Amos!" Mr. Auld shouted. "Get out here!"

Amos appeared behind Mr. Auld almost immediately. The old slave gasped when he saw Frederick.

"Take him to the barn and clean him up," Mr. Auld told Amos. He looked down at Frederick. "In the morning, you will return to Covey's, and you will continue to work for him until you learn how to behave."

"I can't, sir," Frederick said. "He whips me every day for nothing."

"Covey doesn't whip slaves unless they need it, Frederick," Mr. Auld said. "You remember that!"

"Sir, I—" Frederick started to say.

But Mr. Auld stopped him with, "And if I see you're still here in the morning, then I'll whip you myself, and I'll make sure it's something you remember."

Frederick knew it was useless to say anything else. Amos reached down and lifted

Frederick so Frederick could put his arms around the man's shoulders. Together, they started toward the barn.

When they were out of earshot, Amos said, "You've got to learn, boy, that if you don't do what the master says, you'll always have trouble."

"I won't always have trouble, Amos," Frederick said. "I will be free someday."

Neither one said another word after they reached the barn. Amos gently helped Frederick undress, then he sponged him off and applied salve to his wounds. Afterward, Amos made Frederick a bed in the hay and covered him up with one of his blankets. Shortly afterward, Amos returned with some food and some newer clothes.

"Thank you, Amos," Frederick said.

"You can thank me if you're gone before Mr. Auld gets up," Amos said. "If he sees you wearing these clothes, he'll know I stole them, and then I'll be in trouble too, and I'm too old to be whipped anymore."

"I'll be gone," Frederick said.

After Amos left, Frederick lay in the hay, letting the salve work its way into the wounds and the food digest, and then he quietly but quickly got up and left the barn. He knew if he stayed there, he'd probably sleep until Mr. Auld was already up and about, and he didn't want to get Amos in trouble. He remembered a place near one of the small streams a few miles back down the road, on the way to Covey's farm, where he could rest under a bush until he awakened.

The sun was higher than Frederick had planned it to be when he finally opened his eyes, but he was more rested than he had been in months, and he still felt full from the food Amos had given him. Slowly, he stood up and started back down the road toward the Covey farm.

Frederick had only gone a couple of miles, he calculated, when all the strength in his body seemed to evaporate. Still, he struggled on. He knew that Mr. Auld was not above taking his carriage to Covey's farm to make sure that Frederick had returned.

When Frederick finally rounded a curve in the road and saw Covey's farmhouse in the distance, he also saw Covey walking down the road toward him. He had a whip in his hand.

"I won't let him whip me today," Frederick said. In an angrier voice, he shouted, "I won't! I won't!"

Frederick quickly decided that it would do him no good to run back in the direction of the Aulds' plantation. Instead, he headed to his right, skirted the far edge of a cornfield, away from view of Covey's house, until he came to the woods, and plunged into the trees. Now, he began to feel safe.

Finally, Frederick reached a creek and followed its banks until he found what he thought would be a perfect place to stay for a while. He drank until he was full of the cold, delicious water. When he could hardly keep his eyes open any longer, he lay down, putting his head on some soft moss, and fell asleep.

He was awakened the next morning by a crashing sound. Someone was coming through the thick bushes.

Frederick panicked. He frantically looked around for a place to hide, but by the time he was able to stand up again, a black man appeared and immediately stopped.

"Who are you?" the man demanded.

"Who are you?" Frederick shot back.

The man eyed Frederick warily, then said, "My name is Sandy Jenkins. I'm on my way to see my wife. She's on another farm, about four miles from here."

"My name's Frederick," Frederick said.

"Are you the boy Mr. Covey's been looking for?" Jenkins asked.

Frederick nodded. "How did you know that?" he asked.

"You're not dumb, boy," Jenkins said. He

grinned. "We slaves know everything that's going on around us."

Frederick grinned back. He knew immediately that he could trust this man, so he told him everything that had happened since he had first come to the Covey farm.

Sandy shook his head. "You're in a heap of trouble, boy," he said.

"I know," Frederick said.

"You don't have any other choice but to go back," Sandy told him.

"I'm not going back," Frederick said. "I'm not. I don't know what I'll do, but I'm not going back."

"Why don't you go with me to see my wife, and she'll feed you and get you all cleaned up," Sandy said, "and then we'll talk about what you're going to do."

For a minute, Frederick watched a twig that was floating past him, headed downstream. He suddenly wished he were small enough to be riding on it, going where it was going, out to the ocean and then to Africa, which he only knew from the stories he had heard from some of the old slaves back at Great House Farm. He watched the twig until it disappeared, then he looked up at Sandy and said, "I'll go with you."

Sandy led Frederick through the woods on a trail that only became visible when Sandy pointed out different landmarks.

"I slip over to see my wife when I can," Sandy said. "We have two children, and I want to make sure they always remember their father."

Hearing Sandy's story made Frederick remember how his own mother had made the trip to stay with him when he was just a baby. At that moment, he vowed to make sure that he would not only be free one of these days but that he would never have to slip away to see his children only for a few minutes.

The shack in which Sandy's family lived was just beyond a tree line, so it was easy for

Sandy and Frederick to slip inside without anyone noticing.

Frederick was sure that Sandy's wife would be happy to see her husband, but she made Frederick feel right at home too. She cleaned him up and put salve on his wounds, which had reopened. She also gave him some food. It was only after he had eaten that Frederick realized that his food had actually been Sandy's wife's portion of food. Now she'd be hungry tonight, but it didn't seem to bother her. He would remember her kindness.

When Sandy finally explained why Frederick was there, his wife echoed what Sandy had told Frederick earlier. "You have no choice, Frederick," she said. "We all know who Mr. Covey is, and he will prevail, I can tell you that for the truth."

"You have no choice, Frederick," Sandy repeated. "You have to go back."

• • •

When Sandy left to return to his home, Frederick went with him. When they reached a place where Sandy thought Frederick could get to his shack without being seen, he bid him good-bye.

"We have no choice," Sandy said again. "We have no choice."

Frederick wanted to argue with Sandy, but the man had been too good to him, and he realized that perhaps Sandy really did have no other choice. He had a wife and children. It would have been almost impossible for them to escape, he decided.

"Thank you, Sandy," Frederick said. "I'll never forget you."

"Go, boy," Sandy said.

Frederick left the security of the thick stand of trees and headed across a field toward the shack. He had almost made it to the door when Mr. Covey suddenly came around a corner of the building.

Frederick stopped. His first inclination was

to run back to the woods, but he knew that would only delay what was going to happen to him, so he was thoroughly puzzled when Mr. Covey simply turned around and walked away.

As Frederick watched Covey disappear, he made a life-changing decision. *Never again will I allow Mr. Covey or anyone else to beat me!*

Instead of going inside the shack, Frederick decided he would simply start doing his chores again. He headed toward the stables to see if Covey's horses needed any feed or water. From what he could see, it looked as though no one had fed them today, so Frederick dragged a burlap bag of feed from a store-room and filled each trough with it. Next, he pumped water into the water trough in each stall.

Just as he finished, Frederick felt a strong arm around his neck.

"You didn't think you'd get punished, did

you, boy?" Covey asked. "Well, you were wrong. You were *dead* wrong."

Frederick immediately whirled around, out of Covey's hold, and was now face-to-face with the slave breaker. A surprised Covey tried to step back, but Frederick grabbed him.

"What's wrong with you, boy?" Covey demanded. "You're just asking to be killed!"

"You're never going to whip me again, Covey!" Frederick shouted.

When Covey opened his mouth, Frederick threw a punch, which bloodied Covey's lower lip.

"You little. . . ," Covey tried to say, but Frederick threw another punch, causing Covey to fall to the ground.

Frederick jumped on him, and soon, they were rolling through the barn. Frederick would throw a punch, then Covey would throw a punch, but in the end, Frederick's youth was too much for the slave breaker.

"All right! All right!" Covey cried. "Stop it!"

"Why?" Frederick demanded.

"I can't take it! I give up!" Covey moaned. "I won't whip you again."

Frederick was sure he hadn't heard Covey right, so he said, "Shout it out, Mr. Covey! Shout it so loud that the whole world can hear you!"

When Covey hesitated, Frederick reared back his arm as if to punch Covey in the face again, so Covey quickly shouted, "I won't ever whip you again!"

Frederick released Covey and backed a few feet away from him. He was prepared for Covey to come at him again, but all Covey did was pick himself up, dust himself off, and stalk out of the barn. Frederick watched the man disappear around the corner of the barn, then he fell to his knees, exhausted.

"Oh, what have I done?" he moaned. "He'll find a way to kill me for sure now."

Frederick was wrong, though. Edward Covey never touched him again. In fact, Covey made a point to stay away from him. Frederick never said anything to the other slaves about what had happened, and they never said anything to him, but he thought he noticed a change in their attitude toward him.

Months later, Frederick finally decided to ask a slave named John. "Is he afraid of me?" Frederick whispered to him one evening.

John scratched his white beard and thought for a moment. "I can't say for sure that he's afraid of *you*, Frederick," he said, "but I do know for a fact that he's afraid of what might happen if people ever find out."

"What do you mean?" Frederick asked.

"Covey's supposed to be a slave breaker," John explained, "so his reputation would be ruined if all these white folks around found out that one of the slaves he was supposed to break actually won a fight with him."

Frederick thought for a minute. Then he grinned. "I hadn't thought about that," he said. "I guess you're right."

That night, when Frederick lay down, he knew there was no turning back for him now. He had stood up to a slave breaker. He had refused to be broken, and he had won. This was another step on the road to becoming a freeman.

Two days later, when Frederick was feeding the horses, he noticed a shadow behind him, and he quickly whirled around. His heart sank. "Mr. Covey!"

"Go pack your belongings, Frederick," Covey said. "Mr. Auld has hired you out to work on William Freeland's farm. I want you to leave as soon as possible. You'll find the farm—"

"I know where it is, Mr. Covey," Frederick interrupted.

Covey blinked.

Frederick knew that Covey wanted to know how he knew, but there was no way he was going to tell the man anything. Still, he couldn't get over his good fortune to learn he'd be working on the same farm where his friend Sandy Jenkins worked.

# We'll Escape on Easter Sunday

Before dawn on January 1, 1834, Frederick left the Covey farm and started down the road toward the farm of William Freeland. Frederick had already learned as much as he could about his new master. Even though Mr. Freeland wasn't as wealthy as some of the other landowners, he was an educated gentleman and, from all accounts, was said to be honest and treated all people—even slaves— with respect.

The first person Frederick saw, just as the

sun was coming up, was Sandy Jenkins. "I've come to live here," he told his friend.

"We heard that news," Sandy said. "I'm glad for you."

"Is it true, Sandy, all they say about Mr. Freeland, that he's unlike most slave owners?" Frederick asked.

Sandy scratched his chin for a minute, then said, "Well, Mr. Freeland only owns two slaves, Henry and John Harris. The rest of us, you, Handy Caldwell, and myself, of course, have been hired out to him, and he treats us all well, but . . ." Sandy stopped and scratched his chin again.

"What?" Frederick said, all prepared for news he thought he really didn't want to hear.

"It's just not the same as being free," Sandy finally said, "and that's what we all want someday."

Frederick nodded. "And I truly think it'll happen too," he said.

Sandy shrugged. "Maybe. Maybe not. Anyway, come on, and I'll show you around," he said.

The minute he stepped onto Mr. Freeland's land, Frederick was sure he could tell a difference. Sandy took him to the quarters he would be sharing with the other men, and as soon as he entered the door, he heard people laughing. It had been a long time since he had heard that sound. Sandy introduced Frederick to everyone. The men shook hands with him, told him they were glad he was there, and showed him where he would be sleeping.

Outside, Frederick heard a bell ringing. "What's that?" he asked.

"We need to get a move on," Sandy said. "We've all got chores to do—including you!" He grinned. "First, though, we need to let Mr. Freeland know you're here."

"Let him eat something first, Sandy," John Harris said. "I'll bring him along with me."

Frederick remembered that John was one of the two slaves that Mr. Freeland owned, but he certainly didn't sound anything like the other slaves he knew. He sounded like someone who made his own decisions.

Frederick's breakfast consisted of some of the lightest biscuits he had ever eaten, some gravy thick with lard, and a slice of pork. There was also a lot of strong black coffee.

"You need your nourishment to do good work, Frederick," John said, "and Mrs. Freeland insists we all eat as well as Mr. Freeland can afford."

"I'm not used to this, John," Frederick said. "Some days at Mr. Covey's, I didn't have anything to eat."

At the mention of Covey's name, John spat on the dirt floor. "That's what I think of that slave breaker."

When Frederick finished eating, John stood up and said, "We need to be getting along."

149

He handed Frederick a heavy coat and some gloves. "Put these on. They'll keep you warm."

Frederick drained the rest of his coffee, put on the coat and gloves, and followed John out the door. "At all the other places I've been, John, the masters didn't care if we were cold or not."

"Things are different here, Frederick," John said. "I say my prayers every night for my good fortune."

Frederick vowed he would too.

Mr. Freeland was talking to Sandy and the two other men when Frederick and John walked up.

"Well, there's my new worker," Mr. Freeland said. He smiled and stuck out his hand for Frederick to shake.

Frederick shook it and smiled back. "Yes, sir, I'm sorry if I'm late, but I was eating, and I—"

Mr. Freeland held up his hand. "There's

no need to apologize, son. My workers know what I expect from them, and they give it to me, and we all get along just fine." He turned to Sandy. "You can show Frederick here what we need to get done today. Maybe we can take care of it before it starts to snow. Let's try."

As it turned out, they were only able to repair half of the fence in a far pasture before the snow started falling so heavily that it was hard to see, so Sandy called a halt to the work, and they all started back to their quarters.

They were almost there when they met Mr. Freeland coming toward them. "I was wondering where you all were," he said. "You should probably have started back sooner. I think we're going to be in for quite a time with this storm." Mr. Freeland turned to Sandy. "There's a big jug of hot cider waiting for you on the porch. Mrs. Freeland thought it would warm you up."

"Thank you, sir," Sandy said. He looked at

Frederick. "It'll be heavy. Why don't you help me carry it?"

Frederick nodded. The thought of being inside with the other men and drinking hot cider while it snowed outside sounded heavenly to him.

For the rest of that day, the men stayed inside, drinking the hot cider and eating a hot meal that Mrs. Freeland prepared for them later. It had been so long since Frederick had felt this good about anything, it almost came as a surprise when Handy Caldwell started talking about wanting his freedom.

"Why are you so unhappy with your life here, Handy?" Henry demanded.

"I don't think there's anything wrong with wanting to be free, Henry," Frederick said. "I started thinking about escaping when I was living in Baltimore. In fact, many times since, I've wished I had, so I wouldn't have had to live with Master Thomas Auld or Master

Edward Covey." He looked around. "Still, I sometimes wonder what will be waiting for me," he added.

"Most white people in the south aren't like the Freelands," Sandy said. "You'd have to go to a northern state to find white people who would help us start a new life."

"What if we got caught? What would happen to us then?" Henry said. "No, sir, we've got it too good here."

"You call this good?" Handy said.

"Yeah, I call this good," Henry replied.

Frederick told the men what he had heard about the Underground Railroad. "If other slaves can do it," he said, "we can too."

"I don't care about any Underground Railroad," Handy said. "I just want to get to Baltimore, and then I'm going to find a ship that'll take me to anywhere in Europe."

"Ireland's in Europe," Frederick said. "I talked to two men from there in Baltimore harbor, and they told me that slavery is wrong."

153

For several minutes, no one spoke, then John said, "If I ever decide to escape, that's where I'd go too, Europe, because there are men in the northern states who kidnap black men, free or not, and take them back down south to sell."

"Well, I've heard stories about that happening in Europe, too, brother," Henry said, "so that's why you and I are going to stay here."

"It would be really hard for me to do it, because I have a wife and children," Sandy said. "There's probably no way a whole family could escape together."

Frederick looked at him. "There might be," he said. "I don't think any of you should give up on the idea of being free."

It snowed heavily almost every day for the next week. Cold winds blew fiercely from the north and froze the snow that had fallen. Not only could Frederick and the other men not work, they could hardly leave their quarters, but once a day, two of them would venture out to gather firewood and to get the food that Mrs. Freeland faithfully prepared for them.

Every one of the men slept a lot, Frederick included, and when they were awake, they often played games, most of them made up on the spur of the moment and using whatever they could find inside the house or out: pebbles, sticks, or pieces of wire.

They also planned their escape to freedom.

"We'll have to get passes," Sandy told them.

Frederick looked at him. "What do you mean?" he asked.

"You've never heard about passes before?" Henry said. "It's a piece of paper that says you can travel outside the plantation. Your master writes out that you have permission to do what you're doing. If you don't have it, you're in a lot of trouble."

"Any white person can stop you and ask to see your pass too," Handy said. "And you have to show it to them."

"How are we going to get passes?" John asked.

"I'll make them," Frederick told them. "I know how to write."

The men gave him an astonished look.

"I also know how to read," Frederick added. He gave the men a big grin. "Now, all we have to do is decide *when* we're going to escape."

After a lot of lively talk over the next few weeks, they all decided that the best time to travel would be Easter.

"It's a very important holiday for white people," Handy said. "They dress up for church and they go visiting. They won't think too much about slaves having passes to do the same thing."

From time to time, both Henry and John helped Mrs. Freeland with some of the household chores, so they knew where Mr. Freeland kept his writing paper and ink quills. It was easy for them to steal several sheets of vellum and a quill for Frederick to use for the passes.

Over the next few days, after the men had come in from the fields, they would put a small table in a corner of a room, away from the windows, and set a lamp on it so Frederick could work on the passes.

"You'll only need four passes, Frederick," Sandy told him. "My wife is afraid for the children. We're not going."

Frederick looked at him. "You'll probably be punished when they find out what happened," he said.

"I'll just have to take my chances," Sandy said. "Mr. Freeland is a good man, and he will be very angry, but I think he'll direct that anger at you, not at me."

"I hope so," Frederick said.

The passes were finished on time, and Frederick was extremely proud of them. He was sure that any white person looking at the documents would think that only a white person could have written them.

At dawn, on the Saturday before Easter, Frederick, Handy, John, and Henry could hardly contain their excitement, but they knew that they had to act as though it were simply another day. They were fortunate in that Mr. Freeland didn't expect them to do very much work on most Saturdays, and, with the spring crops planted, he didn't care if the men headed toward the creek to do a little fishing. That was the plan. Sandy had even dug some worms for them, and had the five cane poles leaning up against the corner of the house.

"Just as we start to leave, I'll get sick," Sandy had told them, "and I'll tell the four of you to go on."

When a horn sounded letting the men know that breakfast was ready, Frederick said, "I'm going to go ahead, like I usually do, so they won't suspect anything. We need to act as though this is just a normal day."

The other men agreed.

Frederick stepped out onto the small stoop, took a deep breath of the spring air, and then headed toward the kitchen, at the rear of the Freeland house, where Mrs. Freeland always set out the men's food on a long, rough wooden table. He was almost there when he saw Mr. Freeland coming from the barn. A slave named Hamilton, from a neighboring farm, and two policemen were following him.

Frederick felt his blood go cold. His instinct was to run back to the shack to warn the others, but he knew that would only make him look guilty, so he continued toward the backdoor, acting as though nothing was wrong. To make matters worse, he had his fake pass on him, as would Handy, John, and Henry when they came to breakfast.

"Frederick!" Mr. Freeland called. "Stop! Stay where you are!"

Frederick stopped. *Stay calm,* he told himself. "Yes, sir, Mr. Freeland?" he asked.

Just then, John, Henry, and Handy walked up behind him. He turned and looked at them, and he hoped they could read the expression he had on his face, telling them to act as normal as possible.

"Go on inside," Mr. Freeland said.

Since Mr. Freeland and the policemen were now between them and the backdoor, Frederick realized that they had to follow his orders. Frederick opened the backdoor and stepped inside. The fireplace at the end had a roaring fire in it that had always been so welcoming before, but now it seemed to suck all of the air out of the room.

All of a sudden, though, Frederick had an idea. He headed toward the fireplace.

"Where are you going?" Mr. Freeland demanded.

"To warm myself, sir," Frederick said. He knew Mr. Freeland meant for him to stop, but he kept going. When he reached the fire-place, he managed to pull the pass out of his pocket, without anyone seeing him do it, he hoped, and quickly turn his back to the fire. He flipped the pass, now wadded into a ball, into the fire, and stood where he was sure no one could see it burning. Without the pass on him, there would be no real evidence that he had planned to escape.

Now he had to figure out how to get John, Henry, and Handy to destroy their passes too.

"Tell me about the escape, Frederick," Mr. Freeland said.

"Sir?" Frederick said.

"Don't act dumb, boy," Mr. Freeland said. "We know all about it." He turned to Hamilton. "All the slave owners hereabouts, except me, it seems, know about your plan to escape to Baltimore."

*Who would have told them?* Frederick wondered. *It couldn't have been. . . .* His breath caught. It had to have been Sandy's wife. He couldn't believe that she would have told anyone on purpose, but she could have mentioned it to someone she thought she could trust.

All of a sudden, John shouted, "Run!"

Mr. Freeland and the two policemen were momentarily caught off guard, so without thinking, Frederick sprinted toward the door, but Hamilton managed to trip him, and he fell in front of the door, blocking the escape route. Within seconds, the policemen had tied him up along with John and Handy, but Henry continued to struggle with them.

While Henry and one of the policemen rolled around on the floor, the other policeman pulled his gun and said, "I'll shoot you if you don't stop!"

"Shoot me, then!" Henry shouted. "I can only die once!"

With Henry distracted, the other policeman was able to get his arm around Henry's neck and subdue him. Soon, he was tied up along with Frederick and the others.

"What's going to happen to us, Mr. Freeland?" John asked.

"You're going to jail, that's what," Mr. Freeland said.

Just then, Mrs. Freeland came into the room and said, "John and Henry and Handy aren't going anywhere until they've had something to eat!" She looked over at Frederick. "You did this to them, you with your conniving ways. I told my husband it was a mistake to bring you here. Mrs. Covey told me she thought you were evil, and now I agree with her."

As the policemen untied the three men's hands so they could eat, Frederick managed to say, "Put the passes inside the biscuits and eat them so they won't be found."

Frederick wasn't given any food, but he did see that John and Henry did as he had suggested, so now there was no real evidence about their planned escape.

When the three men had finished eating, they, along with Frederick, were taken outside and tied to a team of horses so they could be dragged along the road to the jailhouse.

When they finally reached the jailhouse, the four of them were put inside one cell.

"I'm sorry," Frederick said.

"I don't blame you, Frederick," Henry told him.

"In fact, this has made me want my freedom even more," Handy added.

"Me too," John agreed. "If someone like Mr. Freeland can do this, then we can't trust any white man."

Just then, the cell door opened. Mr. Freeland was standing there with a policeman. Frederick froze. *What are they going to do to us?* he wondered.

"Get up, John. Get up, Henry. Get up, Handy," Mr. Freeland said. "You're going home."

"What about Frederick, sir?" John asked.

"He's staying in jail," Mr. Freeland said, "and I don't care if he rots here."

Frederick stayed in jail for another week, wondering almost every moment what was going to happen to him, thinking the worst, especially when he would hear angry voices outside the small window.

Finally, on a Sunday, just as it was beginning to get light, Thomas Auld appeared with a policeman, who opened the cell door.

"Stand up!" the policeman shouted at Frederick.

Frederick obeyed and then followed the two men to a backdoor, where a buggy was tied up.

"Get up on the seat beside me, Frederick," Mr. Auld said. "We're going back to St. Michaels."

Again, Frederick did as he was told, but he waited until they had left the village before he said anything to Mr. Auld. "Thank you for coming for me, sir."

"I was afraid I'd lose the money I have invested in you if I didn't," Mr. Auld said. "I was told that the local community was so angry about what you did that they wanted to kill you as an example to other slaves who might be planning to escape."

Frederick bowed his head. He wondered if Mr. Auld would send him back to Mr. Covey's again. He couldn't survive another stay there, he was sure. For a moment, he thought about jumping out of the buggy and then running and running until he could run no more.

Just then, Mr. Auld said, "I'm sending you back to live with my brother Hugh in Baltimore, Frederick. That'll give me time to decide what I want to do with you next."

It took Frederick a moment to grasp what he had just been told. "Thank you, sir," he finally said.

Frederick couldn't believe his good fortune, and he knew in his heart that this time he would not miss his chance to be free at last.

# Free at Last!

For the first three days that Frederick was back at the Aulds' in Baltimore, it was easy for him to believe that he had never left. The cook gave him a big hug, fed him a huge meal, and Thomas let Frederick look at the different books he was reading in school. Frederick was happy.

On the fourth day, though, Frederick realized that his life in Baltimore wouldn't be exactly like the life he had had before.

"We no longer need your help rearing

Thomas," Mrs. Auld told him. "You were quite useful, when you lived with us before, but Thomas is older now, Frederick, and he can take care of himself."

"Yes, ma'am," Frederick said.

"You'll be expected to work outside our home, Frederick," Mr. Auld chimed in. "I knew they always need strong young men in Baltimore harbor, so I talked to Mr. William Gardner, one of the most important shipbuilders in Maryland, and I was able to arrange for you to become his apprentice."

Frederick liked what he was hearing. He enjoyed being around ships, and now he was going to help build them. Working in the harbor would also put him in contact with people who could help him escape up north to freedom.

"Thank you, Mr. Auld," Frederick said. "I appreciate that very much."

"Of course, since we'll be the ones providing you with room and board, it'll be necessary for you to turn over your entire wages to me," Mr. Auld added. "I'll expect to receive them at the end of each week."

"Yes, sir," Frederick said. But he had to fight hard not to show his anger. To him, this was one more reason why he wanted to be a freeman. It didn't make any sense for him to work hard and then be forced to give up all of his wages to Mr. Auld. He would not have minded paying Mr. Auld for the food he ate or for the room he slept in, but he did resent giving the man *all* of his wages. Still, he repeated, "Yes, sir."

The next morning, Frederick left the Aulds' house and headed for Baltimore's shipyards. After asking several dockworkers for directions, he finally reached Mr. Gardner's small office.

"You're late," Mr. Gardner said. "If you want to be my apprentice, you'll have to be on time."

"Yes, sir," Frederick said.

Frederick noticed two white boys about his age snickering at each other. He was sure they would cause him problems before the day was over. Still, he was willing to put up with almost anything in order to learn a trade.

Mr. Gardner put Frederick to work right away. He spent the rest of the day carrying timbers from a huge warehouse to dockside, where other workers nailed them to the frame of a ship being built. Several times he noticed that most of the white apprentices were just standing around watching him. At first, he decided to ignore them, but as the day wore on and as he got more and more tired, he asked another black worker why the apprentices weren't doing anything.

"They don't want to work with a black man, Frederick," the man said. "They feel that doing the same job you're doing is beneath them."

•　　•　　•

At sundown, Mr. Gardner told Frederick to carry his last load of timbers back to warehouse, because it was getting too late for the carpenters to do their job.

"And I expect you here in the morning at dawn," Mr. Gardner added. "If you're late, then you might as well not show up."

Frederick wanted to ask him why the white apprentices had left several hours before, but he knew what Mr. Gardner's answer would be, so he held his tongue and said, "Yes, sir."

The next day, Frederick continued to carry timbers from the warehouse to the dockside. In between loads, he saw that the white apprentices were now helping to build teak deckhouses, teak covers to companionways, and masts with spars and rigging.

When Frederick told Mr. Gardner that he'd like to learn other things about shipbuilding too, Mr. Gardner became so angry that he pushed Frederick to the floor and said, "You'll do what I tell you to do."

•　•　•

That night, Frederick decided that he would not complain again to Mr. Gardner. He would complete each task assigned him, no matter what it was, and would always do his work better than the white apprentices. Sooner or later, Frederick was sure, someone on the docks would notice what a good apprentice he was and maybe talk to him about coming to work for them.

The next day, though, try as he might, everything seemed to go wrong. The timbers in the warehouse had been restacked so that when Frederick moved them, they almost fell on him. He barely managed to escape being crushed. Frederick knew almost immediately that the white apprentices were responsible. He vowed he wouldn't say a word about it and quickly managed to restack the timbers without losing too much time. Still, he knew the white apprentices wouldn't stop trying to make his life miserable.

At sundown, Frederick stopped work and, gathering up his things, started to leave, but Mr. Gardner blocked his way and said, "Where are you going?"

"Home, Mr. Gardner," Frederick pointed to the sky. "There's no sun, sir. I can't see."

"I'll carry a lamp for you," Mr. Gardner said. "You're not finished until I say you're finished."

With Mr. Gardner lighting his way, Frederick managed to carry two more stacks of timbers to dockside.

"Now, you may go home," Mr. Gardner said.

"Thank you, sir," Frederick told him.

As Frederick left the docks, he thought he saw movement in the darkness ahead of him, but he decided that the moonlight was either playing tricks on his eyes or it was just some stray animal. When he reached the corner of one of the last buildings, though, four of the white apprentices barred his way.

"We're not going to work with a black man any longer," one of them said. He threw a brick at Frederick's face. Frederick dodged but not enough to keep the brick from striking him on the shoulder.

"Well, I'm not quitting," Frederick shouted at them.

Immediately, the four apprentices started toward him. Frederick remembered the promise he had made to himself at Covey's farm, never to be beaten again, so he stood his ground as the four apprentices rushed at him, brandishing large sticks.

Not long after the fight began, though, Frederick knew that he couldn't stand up against such overwhelming odds.

When Frederick became conscious, he felt horrible pains shooting all through his body. He knew that he needed help. After a few minutes, he managed to get to his knees. He crawled a few feet to the edge of the nearest building and then used it to help him stand. He was bloody, and his clothes were in tatters.

It seemed to take an eternity, but he finally reached the Aulds' house. Frederick used the knocker, and then held his breath, which was hard to do, because his chest felt like it was on fire. Mrs. Auld opened the front door. The cook was behind her, holding a lantern.

When Frederick heard her say, "Oh, my poor child, what have they done to you?" he knew that everything would be all right. It was the last thing he remembered before he collapsed again.

When Frederick next awakened, it was midafternoon, and he was lying in his bed, covered with bandages. He had no idea how he had gotten there, but he was sure that it was Mr. Auld who had carried him and that it was Mrs. Auld who had tended to his wounds.

Just then, Mrs. Auld peeked inside his

room. "Oh, you're finally awake. Good. The doctor is here to examine you." She gave him a big smile, just like the one she'd had on her face when he'd first met her. "You're going to be all right, Frederick. I'll make sure nothing like this ever happens to you again."

After Frederick had fully recovered, the Aulds refused to let him return to work for William Gardner.

"I've arranged for you to work for Walter Price," Mr. Auld told him. "He's a good man, and he'll teach you how to caulk ships to make them watertight."

At first, Frederick was nervous. He didn't want to go anywhere near the harbor, for fear of being attacked again by the white apprentices, but Mr. Price's office was almost two miles from Mr. Gardner's, and on the first day that Frederick arrived, two of Mr. Price's white apprentices greeted him with handshakes and immediately started to show him how ships were caulked.

Frederick was sure that things would eventually change, because he had learned not to trust most white men too much. But day after day everyone not only continued to help him hone his caulking skills but also treated him like another human being.

When one of Mr. Price's black men asked him if he'd be interested in joining the East Baltimore Mental Improvement Society, Frederick asked him what it was.

"It's a debating club," the man said. "We talk about all the issues that confront free black men."

"I'm not free," Frederick said. He explained how he came to work for the Aulds. "I could be sent back to the plantation at any time."

"That's all the more reason for you to join, then," the man told him. "It'll open your mind to all kinds of possibilities for your life."

Frederick didn't have to think twice. He attended his first meeting that night.

178

At that first meeting, Frederick met a woman named Anna Murray. Immediately, Frederick knew he was falling in love. Anna was a housekeeper for a prominent Baltimore white family. She was also a free woman.

On the way back to the Aulds' that evening, Frederick made a decision. *I'm going to run away. I'm going to be free.* He took a deep breath and let it out as he turned onto the Aulds' street. *If I don't, I can never have a life with Anna. She would never marry a slave.*

# Life Begins Up North

On September 3, 1838, twenty-year-old Frederick dressed up like a seaman, borrowed some identification papers from a free black sailor, and boarded a train in Baltimore for New York City. If his plan worked, he'd be a freeman, but if it didn't, he'd be back on the plantation, at the mercy of the overseer's whip.

The train was well on its way to the next station by the time the conductor reached the car where Frederick was slouched in a seat, pretending to be asleep.

The conductor shook him by the shoulder and said, "All right, sailor boy, show me your ticket!"

Frederick fumbled around for a minute, pulled a dirty piece of paper from his pocket, and handed it to the conductor.

"Do you have your free papers on you?" the conductor asked.

Frederick forced himself to breathe steadily. "No, sir, I never carry my papers to sea with me," he said. "I don't want to take a chance on losing them."

"Well, you have to have *something* to prove that you're free, boy!" the conductor said angrily. "Show it to me!"

Frederick made himself smile. From his other pocket, he withdrew another paper, unfolded it carefully, and gave it to the conductor. "That little old bird has carried me around the world, sir," he said. At the top of the paper was an American eagle, and the conductor recognized it as a "sailor's protection"

181

issued by the United States government

The conductor glanced at the document, nodded, then returned it.

Frederick tried to keep his hand from trembling as he refolded the paper and put it back in his pocket. If the conductor had really examined it carefully, he would have seen that it actually belonged to a man who had much darker skin than Frederick. Not only would Frederick have been arrested, but so would the sailor who had lent it to him.

Frederick took a deep breath. He knew the danger wasn't over yet. After they left Maryland, the train still had to pass through Delaware, another slave state, where slave catchers could be waiting, so Frederick made a decision. He would get off the train at the next stop and take a boat the rest of the way to New York. He thought there would be less chance of encountering slave catchers that way.

Frederick finally arrived in New York the

next day, a freeman, but he was still afraid that if he talked to people they might know right away that he was an escaped slave and sell him back to a slave catcher. Finally, he made friends who suggested he change his name to Johnson. He did.

A few days later, Anna Murray joined Frederick in New York, and they were married on September 15. Soon afterward, they moved to New Bedford, Massachusetts, where Frederick was able to get jobs sawing wood, sweeping chimneys, and digging cellars. Anna worked by washing and ironing clothes for white people. They lived with a couple named Mary and Nathan Johnson. It was Nathan who suggested that Frederick change his last name to Douglas, after one of the characters in Sir Walter Scott's poem *The Lady of the Lake*. Frederick took Nathan's advice, but he spelled it *Douglass*.

Frederick also tried to get a job in the shipyards as a caulker but, once again, he faced discrimination from white workers who threatened to quit if Frederick was hired, so Frederick continued working whatever odd jobs he could find.

On June 24, 1839, Frederick and Anna's daughter Rosetta was born. Frederick also began to take more of an interest in the work of the abolitionists, people who wanted to get rid of slavery in the United States. He subscribed to William Lloyd Garrison's weekly newspaper *The Liberator*. He also became a licensed preacher for the African Methodist Episcopal Zion Church. The Douglasses welcomed their first son, Lewis Henry, on October 9, 1840.

In 1841 Frederick was invited to speak at an anti-slavery meeting in New Bedford. Later that same year he was asked to speak about his life as a slave at the Massachusetts Anti-Slavery Society Convention. William Lloyd Garrison was present and gave a speech in which he encouraged Frederick to continue his antislavery work. The Society was also impressed by what they saw and hired Frederick as a speaker. Frederick was now a close ally of Garrison and a spokesperson for his abolitionist views.

Another son was born on March 3, 1842. Frederick and Anna named him Frederick, Jr. That year, Frederick became close friends with Charles Lenox Remond, a black abolitionist.

In 1843, after an antislavery meeting in Pendleton, Indiana, Frederick was beaten by a local mob. His right hand was broken, and he never fully regained the use of it.

When a third son was born in 1844, he was named Charles Remond, to honor the abolitionist.

In 1845, while on a speaking tour, Frederick met Susan B. Anthony, and he himself became a champion of women's rights. In order to make money and to show the world the horrors of slavery, Frederick wrote his autobiography, *The Narrative of the Life of Frederick*

*Douglass*. After it was published, though, Frederick realized that he had revealed details that could lead to his arrest as a fugitive slave.

Fearing capture, Frederick began of tour of Great Britain and Ireland with William Lloyd Garrison, lecturing on the evils of slavery. He was gone for two years, during which time English audiences raised enough money to buy Frederick's freedom from Hugh Auld.

When Frederick returned to the United States in 1847, he was truly a freeman. He moved his family to Rochester, New York. Frederick also had enough money left over to buy a printing press with which he began publication of *North Star*, a weekly abolitionist newspaper. He published the newspaper until 1851.

# Abolitionist

In 1848, Frederick went to Seneca Falls, New York, to participate in the nation's first ever women's rights convention. Later that year he became friends with the abolitionist John Brown and began sheltering escaped slaves who were fleeing to the north on the Underground Railroad. Once again, though, Frederick realized that discrimination was everywhere in the United States, not just in the south, when his daughter Rosetta was barred from attending school in Rochester because she was an African American. Immediately, Frederick and his abolitionist friends began a movement to end segregation in the public schools of Rochester.

Another daughter, Annie, was born on March 22, 1849.

In 1851, Frederick merged *North Star* with Gerrit Smith's *Liberty Party Paper* to form *Frederick Douglass' Paper*. He also changed his opinion about the Constitution of the United States. Earlier, he had considered it a "pro-slavery" document, an opinion shared by William Lloyd Garrison. Now, Frederick agreed with Smith that the Constitution was really an "antislavery" document. This change of opinion created a rift between Frederick and Garrison, but it began a period when Frederick saw himself as a leader of the antislavery movement, with his own opinions, not someone who was helping further the opinions of others.

Frederick's second autobiography, *My*

*Bondage and My Freedom*, was published in 1855.

In 1857, in what many Americans viewed as a major setback for the country's abolitionists, the United States Supreme Court ruled in the *Dred Scott* case that African Americans were not American citizens and that the Congress had no authority to restrict slavery in the United States or in any of its territories. Frederick and his followers saw the ruling as a mandate for more aggressive tactics to do away with slavery.

Two years later, Frederick's friend John Brown and some of Brown's fellow abolitionists raided the federal arsenal in Harpers Ferry, then in Virginia, but today in the state of West Virginia. Brown was eventually captured and, in his belongings, authorities found a letter that Frederick had written to him. Fearing he would be arrested as Brown's accomplice, Frederick fled to Canada and then embarked on another lecture tour of England. Brown was tried, found guilty, and then hanged on December 2, 1859.

While Frederick was gone, his daughter Annie died in Rochester in March 1860. Frederick immediately returned to the United States. On his arrival, he learned that he would not be charged in the John Brown Raid.

# A Great American

Abraham Lincoln became president of the United States in March 1861. The U.S. Civil War began the following month. The people who lived in the South wanted their independence. The people who lived in the North wanted all of the states to remain united. Most Americans, including Frederick, believed that the issue of slavery was the main reason for the war.

Frederick worked hard to get African Americans to join the Union army to fight against the Confederate army of the South. He was shocked when most Northerners—including President Lincoln—said they didn't want black soldiers fighting alongside white soldiers. When Frederick asked people why, they told him they didn't think black soldiers would be brave on the battlefields.

In speeches, Frederick told audiences that President Lincoln should be ashamed of his attitude. The Union army needed black soldiers to help win the war. Two years later, Lincoln realized that Frederick was right. African American men were allowed to join the Union army. They weren't allowed to fight, though. They were used to dig trenches for the white soldiers. Frederick was angry and sad at this treatment, but he still wanted African American men in the army because he said this was a way they could show that they deserved to be treated as equals to white people.

Frederick toured New York in the spring

of 1863, urging more African American men to join the Union army. Among the men who heeded his call to enlist were his sons, Charles and Lewis.

When African American soldiers were finally allowed to fight, they immediately showed their bravery. Many of them were either killed in battle or seriously wounded. Some were captured by Confederate troops who beat them, then either killed them or sent them to the South where they were sold into slavery. When Frederick heard about this, he became very angry and asked to speak to President Lincoln.

Frederick had a meeting with Lincoln at the White House in August 1863. Lincoln paid very close attention to Frederick's request that black soldiers be treated as equals to white soldiers. Lincoln told Frederick that this would happen one day—but not right away. Although Frederick wasn't happy with what the president said, he told everyone that

he believed Lincoln was an honest man. After he left the meeting, he immediately set about trying to get more blacks to become soldiers.

Shortly after the Civil War ended in 1865, President Lincoln was assassinated, and Frederick, along with most Americans, was shocked and saddened. Later that year, the Emancipation Proclamation was signed, freeing all slaves, but African Americans weren't given all the rights that white Americans had. Frederick visited with the new president, Andrew Johnson, and told him that blacks needed the right to vote, the same as white people. He also thought blacks should be able to get government jobs.

In 1872, Frederick decided to move his family to Washington, D.C., in hopes of getting a government job himself. In 1877, at the age of fifty-nine, Frederick became a United States Marshall for the District of Columbia, and in 1881, he became one of the District's Recorder of Deeds.

The next year, 1882, Frederick suffered a great loss when his wife, Anna, died, but a year and a half later, he shocked both blacks and whites in the country by marring Helen Pitts, a white woman. Even Frederick's children were angry. Frederick couldn't understand everyone's objections. He had never believed that race should make a difference in relationships. He told people that he and Helen loved each other and that was all that mattered.

In 1889, Frederick was appointed the United States Minister (ambassador) to Haiti. Over the next two years he and Helen traveled around that country, making friends and promoting business deals between Haiti and the United States.

When Frederick and Helen returned to the United States, Frederick continued writing and speaking about the evils of slavery and discrimination among the races. On February 20, 1895, while attending a meeting of the

National Council of Women in Washington, D.C., he collapsed. He was taken to his home, where he later died.

Americans mourned the loss of a great American. Frederick Douglass had used his talents to make the United States a better country for all races.

# For More Information

## BOOKS

Blight, David W. *Frederick Douglass' Civil War: Keeping Faith in Jubilee*. Baton Rouge: Louisiana State University Press, 1991.

Douglass, Frederick, Philip S. Foner (editor), Yuval Taylor (editor). *Frederick Douglass: Selected Speeches and Writings*. Chicago: Lawrence Hill Books, 2000.

Douglass, Frederick. *Narrative of the Life of Frederick Douglass, an American Slave*. New York: Barnes & Noble Books, 2003.

Haugen, Brenda. *Frederick Douglass: Slave, Writer, Abolitionist*. Minneapolis: Compass Point Books, 2005.

McFeely, William S. *Frederick Douglass*. New York: W.W. Norton & Company, 1991.

Preston, Dickson J. *Young Frederick Douglass: The Maryland Years*. Baltimore: The Johns Hopkins University Press, 1985.

Sweeney, Fionnghuala. *Frederick Douglass and the Atlantic World*. Liverpool: Liverpool University Press, 2007.

## WEBSITES

http://memory.loc.gov/ammem/doughtml/
doughome.html
www.history.rochester.edu/class/douglass/home.html
www.nps.gov/frdo/freddoug.html

199

★★★ **Childhood of Famous Americans** ★★★

One of the most popular series ever published for young Americans, these classics have been praised alike by parents, teachers, and librarians. With these lively, inspiring, fictionalized biographies—easily read by children of eight and up—today's youngster is swept right into history.

Abigail Adams
John Adams
Louisa May Alcott
Susan B. Anthony
Neil Armstrong
Arthur Ashe
Crispus Attucks
Clara Barton
Elizabeth Blackwell
Daniel Boone
Buffalo Bill
Ray Charles
Roberto Clemente
Crazy Horse
Davy Crockett
Joe Dimaggio
Walt Disney
Frederick Douglass
Amelia Earhart
Dale Earnhardt
Thomas Edison
Albert Einstein
Henry Ford
Ben Franklin
Lou Gehrig
Geronimo

Althea Gibson
John Glenn
Jim Henson
Milton Hershey
Harry Houdini
Langston Hughes
Andrew Jackson
Mahalia Jackson
Tom Jefferson
Helen Keller
John Fitzgerald Kennedy
Martin Luther King, Jr.
Robert E. Lee
Meriwether Lewis
Abraham Lincoln
Mary Todd Lincoln
Thurgood Marshall
John Muir
Annie Oakley
Jacqueline Kennedy Onassis
Jessie Owens
Rosa Parks
George S. Patton
Molly Pitcher
Pocahontas
Ronald Reagan

Christopher Reeve
Paul Revere
Jackie Robinson
Knute Rockne
Mr. Rogers
Eleanor Roosevelt
Franklin Delano Roosevelt
Teddy Roosevelt
Betsy Ross
Wilma Rudolph
Babe Ruth
Sacagawea
Sitting Bull
Dr. Seuss
Jim Thorpe
Harry S. Truman
Sojourner Truth
Harriet Tubman
Mark Twain
George Washington
Martha Washington
Laura Ingalls Wilder
Wilbur And Orville Wright

★★★ Collect them all! ★★★